PATENT PENDING AND DEATH

Book One: Fleming
Investigations Cozy Mysteries

PATTI LARSEN

Cover design by Christina Gaudet
www.castlekeepcreations.com

Thanks, Kirstin!

ISBN-13: 978-1-988700-97-7

CHAPTER ONE

I LOVED MY DESK. I'd bought it just for my corner of the office, the cherry wood finish renewed to gorgeous shine with a soft sanding and a hearty bit of elbow grease and oil. Sure, it was a contrast to Dad's utilitarian metal and plastic, hovering squat and rather unsavory at the far end of the long, narrow space. I was glad mine was closer to the front door, far from the depths of the Fleming Investigations open concept. My desk deserved better than to be compared to what I'm sure Dad bought at a discount sale compared to my antique find lovingly returned to its original glory by yours truly.

Okay, so it was a desk, right? Big deal. Except, it was a big deal to me. I'd never had a desk before. In an office I co-owned in a business I co-founded (yes, Dad roped me into it, but I wasn't arguing, nope), in a job I already loved even though I'd only been at it officially for two months.

Two glorious months, knowing the past was in the past, that everything we'd worked for had finally paid off, that our town, Reading, was safe from conspiracy and a dark history we'd uncovered.

(If you haven't read the **Fiona Fleming Cozy Mysteries**, beginning with *Bed and Breakfast and Murder*, you can continue with *Patent Pending and Death* without the worry of spoilers for the previous series. However, I do recommend you take the time to go to the beginning of Fee's story—I promise you won't be disappointed!)

I'd spent the intervening time studying diligently for my P.I. license, temporary registration almost up as my sixty days supervised by my father and husband came to a close. I shuffled some papers, shunting them aside as the door chime welcomed my expected guest. I smiled and rose, circled to shake Jared's hand, the young owner of Wilkins Construction restored in my life along with his new bride, Alicia.

Petunia huffed her dissatisfaction he failed to greet her first, and when he bent to pat my fat pug she farted rather ceremoniously as though following through on her displeasure, so he'd know just where he'd gone wrong.

Jared laughed though I waved at the air between us. Despite the fact I no longer had a bed and breakfast, the establishment that shared her name burned down last year, she still managed to wrangle foods not conducive to a healthy digestive tract thanks to her time spent at my mother's feet at the remains of the business she and I once shared.

"Thanks for coming in," I said, gesturing for him to sit across from me. Jared spread the plans out in front of him, smiling at my eagerness while Toby Miller peeked across from her receptionist station near the door. I waved her over, beaming over the house Crew and I chose to build on the very spot where Petunia's had once stood.

Children. He'd mentioned children when he broached the idea of having a house on that very spot, one where we could share our happily ever after. That's why there were four bedrooms.

Did he really expect to fill them?

"This looks perfect, Jared." I hugged myself, smiling, unable to suppress the wave of wonder and joy that washed over me. Was it only four years ago I came home to the cutest town in America, lost and alone and not sure what to expect of my life in this place where I'd grown up? Who knew I'd be married to the most amazing man in the world, building a new life, a new house, a new career and loving every second of it?

I guess good things did happen to good people.

"Happy to hear you approve of the changes." He rolled up the plans, the shift of the small powder room to just outside the large kitchen exactly what I wanted. "I'll run this down to town planning, but since the change was minor, we're still on target to break ground next week."

Next. Freaking. Week.

Awesome.

"Thank you so much." I rose and hugged him, Petunia receiving her own loving as he crouched this time despite the threat of smelly assault and scratched her ears. The elderly pug groaned her pleasure at the attention. She'd been more active when I'd moved back and taken her as part of my Grandmother Iris's bequeathment, the bed and breakfast I'd inherited part and parcel with the chubby creature at my feet. Poor Petunia had been through a lot in the past year, and though she was only nine, she was definitely slowing down. I tried not to think about it as Jared stood. No matter how long I had with her, I'd decided she'd remain a pampered princess who got her own way.

"How's the detective business treating you?" Jared waited for me to lead him toward the door which I did, pausing at the exit, looking out into the bustling, sunny street. Tourist season hadn't slowed down a bit and with the supposed shoulder season of September as busy as the middle of July, things didn't appear to have changed much even though, well, everything had changed.

At least for the people I cared the most about.

"Great," I said, meaning it, not a hint of sarcasm behind the word. So great. "My forty hours of training are done, firearms tests wrapped up." I still couldn't believe I was going to be able to carry a gun.

I know it made Crew nervous. Speaking of nervous, I didn't mention the fact I was technically required to have two years of experience in investigation before applying. Dad had laughed, citing the multiple murder cases I'd solved and brushed off any arguments I might have had I should wait it out.

Then again, I hated waiting. Patience and I had never been friends. Or passing acquaintances.

"I hear you're handling the local stuff." The tall, handsome young man grinned at me. "Mrs. Porter said you saved her candy store in a half-hour on the job."

Well, it wasn't hard to figure out the two girls she'd hired were eating up her profits. "I'm happy to help," I said. "Dad and Crew have their hands full with bigger cases and since I'm the newbie..." I shrugged, grinned back, though the tweaking annoyance they ran cases without me, and didn't always tell me what they were up to seemed willing to ruin my good humor. I, however, chose not to let it, instead finding my happy all over again. "It's fun, Jared. Really fun. Is that wrong?"

He laughed and hugged me, an uncharacteristic gesture for him, though not unwelcome. We still suffered a little bit of distance, thanks to issues with his family and the adventures of the last four years. But Jared had been my friend pretty much since I got home to Reading, he a frustrated son of a not-so-honest land developer and me a new business owner with problems of my own. I'd missed him, missed Alicia, and it was nice to hug him and feel the stress and separation vanish when he made the first move to clear the air.

"Come for dinner," he whispered. "You and Crew. We'd love that."

"You got it," I said, clearing my throat first so he wouldn't hear the tears in my voice.

He let me go, smiled down at me. "Thanks for trusting me with your dream, Fee. I'll build you the best house you've ever seen. Just wait and see." And, with that, he left, the door chiming at his departure, my heart singing, too.

Best life ever.

I returned to my desk and the recumbent pug who watched me with her big, brown eyes but didn't try to move aside from a tail waggle at my return. There was a time she would have followed me to the door, the ticking of her claws reminding me she was always in need of a mani-pedi. Not thinking about her slow decline. Not.

Fee, *not*.

What was with me, suddenly emotional like this? I hid my wave of sorrow mixed with stuttering nervousness as I perused the stack of files before me. Okay, so it wasn't so new, my state of heightened feels. I'd been struggling a little, I admit. So much had changed and I still felt a bit raw and unprepared for the job. With Dad and Crew out of town so much, and Liz phasing out of the FBI to increase our numbers, it seemed like I was on my own a lot more than I'd expected. And their tendency to cut me out of the details of their cases came back all over again, that lingering resentment understandable from both ends.

Until I had a full license, there were things, Dad told me, I was better off not knowing. Okay, I got that. If something happened, they needed to know they had their ducks in a row and not flying off in odd directions.

Still, I was his partner, by his choice. And I really wanted to know everything.

This was his fault, anyway. He gave me the nosy gene. The problem was, being on my own was the worst part. Yes, having all the insider info would be sweet when the time came. But I'd really hoped we'd be a team, that I'd be part of their collective. Desk duty and minor cases weren't what I'd had planned when I agreed to this.

Working solo wasn't exactly a massive shift or anything. I'd run my own business before. Except, I'd brought on two partners when I'd expanded the bed and breakfast, and now, as I sat there at my coveted cherry desk, I accepted what was really wrong.

Wrong wasn't the right word. Unsettled. I was used to having Mom around, my best friend, Daisy Bruce, both partners in my previous endeavor. I missed them, missed the guests and the cycle of staff through the annex and Petunia's, missed the hustle and bustle of the busy season—who was I kidding, it was always busy in Reading—and the constant call to put out fires.

This job was more interesting, more up my alley,

truth be told. But the rather sedate pace along with only Toby for quiet company—not counting the ever-present but now equally quiet Petunia—took a bit to get used to.

Not that I was craving excitement—outing a pair of teenagers for devouring chocolates they didn't pay for wasn't exactly the level of thrilling crimefighting I was accustomed to—but, well. Yeah.

Excitement, please.

Oh, Fee. Be ever so careful what you wish for.

The phone rang. I answered it. Wished, in retrospect, I'd let it go to voicemail.

"Fiona Fleming?" Whoever my caller was, he didn't wait for me to reply. "This is Lance Dustin with the Vermont Board of Private Investigative and Security Services in Montpelier." Again, no waiting, though I managed to mutter a greeting as he forged on. "There's an issue with your application and we're considering not granting you a license until you answer our questions."

Wait. What?

Oh. Crap.

CHAPTER TWO

THIS COULDN'T BE HAPPENING. Not now, not after everything I'd gone through. I stuttered, unable to come up with a comprehensive reply as Mr. Lance Jerkface went on.

"It's been brought to our attention there are irregularities with your application." Didn't he just sound self-satisfied and like he was riding a high horse I hoped threw him and did some damage? "Namely, your two years of experience as an investigator and whether you are being sufficiently supervised during your sixty-day temporary term." The sound of keys clicking told me he was typing on the other end of the line, noting what, exactly? Details about what he was already telling me? "Since I can only be assured you're following correct procedure by observing in person, I'll be arriving in Reading," he pronounced it Redding, the closed-minded *bourgeois*, "in the morning and we are going to sit down and have a serious conversation," he didn't add *young lady*, but sounded like he wanted to though he had to be younger than me if his tone of voice was any indicator, "about your application."

There was nothing I could do, too floored by the call to react with any sort of intelligent reply. Even my ever-present temper seemed to have abandoned me as the PI Board investigator wrapped up his initial salvo into ruining everything I'd ever wanted.

"Please have all paperwork in order and your registered supervisor—one John Fleming, your father, I presume?" That clearly annoyed the crap out of him, the fact my dad signed off on my application, though why I wasn't sure. "He needs to be present, Ms. Fleming. 9AM, your office. Sharp." With that, he added the final insult to the very personal injury. "Have a nice day." And hung up.

Breathless, hands shaking, I set the cordless handset on my desk, sitting back, knowing I had to be white as a sheet, especially since Toby's wide gaze and open mouth were aimed in my direction.

"Fee," she breathed, her fleece vest tight as she drew a deep, worried breath. "What's wrong?"

I could have lost it then and there, freaked out and cried and thrown things, stomping around the office in a hissy fit of epic proportions that would have likely ended in me running home and burying myself under the covers with a bag of chips and a giant tub of ice cream. At least, the old me might have.

This Fiona Fleming? She'd been through the wars before, thank you very much, and no bitter, misguided and clearly power-hungry, nasty piece of work was going to put an abrupt and final end to the chance I had to live the life I always wanted.

"It's nothing," I said, proud my voice didn't crack, that my body settled into calm, how I held my temper and my hope in a safe and protected space deep inside. "I'm going to head home, though. Let me know if anything comes up and I can be right back." Yes, it was only 4PM and our office hours ended at 5PM, but as confident as I was in my present state of collected professionalism? Yeah, there were no promises any kind of additional conflict layered on top of what just happened wouldn't trigger the previously mentioned meltdown and I really, really needed a win at the moment.

Toby let me go without comment, waving as I smiled pleasantly, my chubby pug huffing softly next to me, preventing me from hurrying with her pedantic pace. Impatience chewed a small, painful hole inside me, but I persisted, restrained and determined not to heft her twenty-five pounds into my arms and run for cover.

My mind's intent to return home was circumvented by my heart's need for comfort and so, a few moments and a couple of blocks later, I crossed the street to the annex, the large and beautifully painted new sign Mom had commissioned declaring the previously unnamed inn as The Iris. I loved the new name, had always adored the gorgeous interior, another Jared Wilkins special. While old memories on the not-so-happy end of the spectrum lingered at times, linked to the house this used to be, the renovation and subsequent transformation of the old Munroe place into this stunning location that was the most on-demand residence in Reading was more than enough to paint over the past.

I entered the foyer, the sunlight warm on the stunning hardwood floors, sweeping staircase glowing, bright white and pale gold paint accenting everything and giving the annex—The Iris—a distinctively homey but elegant appeal that I'd cherished from the moment I'd opened her doors.

While Petunia's had been lovely, welcoming, charming in her antique and sky-blue beauty, she'd been more of an elderly lady whose wrinkles were far more endearing than ugly, her smile as bright as ever, though her wardrobe grown lackluster with time. The Iris, on the other hand, still shone with optimism and freshness, the love and care put into the design evident in every detail, from the scrollwork in the crown moldings to the intricate caps on the corners of each doorway to the burnished brass and copper fittings and crystal chandelier. And that was just the entry.

A pang of loss and nostalgia wasn't helping matters much, making me ache for less complicated times, though I admitted as Petunia led me through the foyer toward the back of the house, passing a few smiling guests on their way out who just had to take a moment and give her a scratch (to her momentary delight, though she had a destination in mind and would not be distracted for long), things were pretty complicated when it came to Petunia's and the annex, too, if I was going, to be honest.

My pug's lack of concern for my future wasn't lost on me, the way her energy picked up and she tugged on her leash, panting, dark eyes white around the edges clear indication she knew exactly where we were going, and I was impeding the joy at the end of our destination making me smile. At least something did.

How had my amazing day become so freaking dark and horrible with one simple phone call?

We passed through the gorgeous dining room, already set up for dinner with the large garden doors open to the warmth of the afternoon, the scent of flowers from the yard filling the space with the last kiss of summer. Petunia's claws scrabbled on the tile floor as she pushed her way through the swinging door and into the kitchen.

Mom turned with a big smile blooming, her flour-covered hands going to the damp towel next to her, the prim, white apron she wore over her pink dress spotless despite the fact I was positive from the smells of sugar and deliciousness that enveloped me she'd spent the last several hours baking. Now that Mom was running things on her own, I was surprised she didn't lighten her own load by hiring out to French's Handmade Bakery. Vivian French, owner and operator of said bakery and newly rediscovered friend I once called an enemy, would have been delighted to supply Mom with whatever she needed. Especially now, with all the water under the bridge we'd burned behind us flowing in happy burbling. But I also knew Mom's passion for cooking and baking was about as powerful as her love for me and Dad and giving up that part of her joy?

Over Lucy Fleming's dead body. Considering she'd almost lost that love once, I figured she'd never give it up again.

"Fee, sweetie." Mom came to my side, kissed my cheek, bent and patted Petunia who panted up at her with the level of eager anticipation on her fat pug face that informed me my mother was part of the pug's food addiction problem and had been enabling her despite my requests to the contrary. "Hello, gorgeous girl," she said to the fat creature at my feet, Petunia groaning her delight when Mom scratched her cheek. "Want a treat, pet?"

The pug yawned one of her cat-like meows and shuffled her feet. A definite yes.

I left her to Mom's tender mercies to greet the second person in the room, Daisy beaming at me as she slipped from the stool where she sat to wrap her arms around me with all her enthusiasm. My bestie might have gone from pauper to princess—not exactly accurate, but close enough—but she didn't lose one scrap of her sunny disposition or the kind openness that was signature Daisy Bruce.

"I'm so happy you're here." She gushed as she let

me go, big, gray eyes sparkling, beautiful face pink with excitement, her flouncy, flowered dress perfectly hugging her gorgeous curves that often made me jealous. She tugged me toward the kitchen island, stainless steel surface pristine everywhere but the precise square of flour Mom used to knead her biscuit dough, sitting me next to her while she slipped a shiny magazine toward me. It was open to the center spread and, as I looked down at the stunning scene with epic flowers and a bride in a sleek, silk dress meant for such a fairy tale, Daisy clutched her hands to her heart and squeaked.

"What do you think?"

I'd come here for comfort, to dump my fear on Mom rather than take it home and deal with it alone. Staring down at my best friend's dream wedding captured in a snapshot carefully designed by those who knew exactly how to make a pending bride lose her freaking mind, I found that need died in a rush of love and excitement for Daisy and her fiancé, and I couldn't have been more grateful.

We spent the next hour giggling together while Mom stole moments from her work to ooh and ahh with us over dress designs, flower arrangements, invitation card stock and more. When Mom's staff finally arrived to begin loading the food she'd created into the dining room for the early dinner shift, I'd almost forgotten all about Lance Dustin and his attitude.

Almost. Honestly, I preferred to focus on my best friend and the stunning man she was marrying.

While not exactly a prince—at least, I didn't think so—Emile Reis was, at the very least, minor European royalty with his faintly French accent and his gorgeous smile, tall enough to be imposing though he never once made me feel uncomfortable, pale blond hair and icy blue eyes giving him that Hollywood perfection I knew I couldn't stand next to for long without feeling inadequate.

Daisy? With her stunning dark curls and exquisite everything? Not to mention her bubbly sweetness? A perfect pairing to his elegant, casual confidence born of nobility and money.

Like, so much money. In fact, he'd bought up every piece of property the Pattersons (Reading's founding family) were forced to sell thanks to their downfall, from the White Valley Ski Lodge and Resort to the old Patterson mansion (despite the fact half of it had been buried in rubble) and the Marie Patterson Olympic Equestrian Center (now renamed the Daisy Chain Equestrian Center, how adorable was that?). Every property, all the bits and pieces of Reading they'd once owned, now in the financial hands of a Luxembourger (that term couldn't be right, could it?) and my own dear, darling Daisy Bruce.

Imagine that?

"How is Emile getting along with Olivia?" The former mayor of Reading, Olivia Walker, had regained her position when Vivian stepped down after the fall of the Patterson family. That meant our tourism efforts were not only back in full swing, but redoubled, Olivia's drive to make the cutest town in America everyone's favorite destination equally annoying and admirable now turned on Daisy's fiancé.

"Oh, he thinks she's adorable." Daisy eye rolled, giggling, while I highly doubted any such term had exited Emile's mouth describing our driven and passionate mayor. "He's loving it here, Fee." Daisy sighed, expression turning to utter devotion and love to the point it was kind of embarrassing and I had my own soul mate. Still, hard to judge her for just how much she adored Emile because every time I saw them together? He was worse.

Like, so much worse. Over-the-top hovering around her sparkly self like a towering, blond mountain of what can I do to make Daisy's life perfect and never, ever let anything bad or hard or sad touch her ever again worse. Which meant, naturally, I adored him, too.

Daisy deserved that kind of love.

Which meant, as my bestie stood to leave, hugging Mom and then me with her particular brand of awesome enthusiasm, I let her go without a word to the wise about my own troubles. And, with my mother's increasing lack of attention on me and focus turned to feeding her guests, I left with a quick embrace and a very disappointed pug—she'd only had one cookie and a handful of strawberries and half a biscuit and three bites of ham and several chunks of cheese, after all, the poor, neglected dear—resolute to figure out my own troubles without my traditional dumping of Fee feelings on the ones I loved.

Yup, this was me, Fiona Fleming, walking my dog home with my head high, my heart light, knowing everything would be fine and I didn't have to talk about what was going on because nothing would come of it and my life was exactly the way it was meant to be.

CHAPTER THREE

FUNNY HOW ALL OF the previous went out the door as I walked in mine to discover my husband was home.

There used to be a time when I would think, "Poor Crew!" having to put up with me and my excessive emotional states. Thing was, he didn't mind, never had, loved me despite my lingering on the edge of meltdowns when things didn't go my way, maybe even partly because of that excessive and eccentric bent I had toward the dramatic.

Still, I did my best to keep from layering him with too much of the previous, if only so I didn't have to feel guilty about always making him the sole inhabitant of my house of horrors. Hard not to, though, when he seemed able, at any given moment, to gauge my mood and whether a storm brewed he was part of, the cause of, or could steer us clear of like he'd been born to wear that compass tattoo on the inside of his right wrist.

Never mind the gold and jewels we thought it had been meant to lead us to. He was the real treasure, thanks.

Crew came right to me though I didn't say a word, taking Petunia's harness off, hanging up her leash, then hugging me tight, lips against my temple, the scent of him as delicious as the first time, all fabric softener and faint musk and coffee tied to hormonal somethings that I would never identify but could pick out in a crowded room.

"Tell me," he said. "We've got this, Fee."

I shook my head, leaned back and actually smiled, a real smile. Because he was right, and you know what? I didn't feel like being miserable before dinner, the yummy smells coming from the kitchen telling me he was making lasagna and fresh bread and a cold beer would be the perfect precursor to such a repast prepared by the man I loved.

"It's fine," I said. "We'll talk after we eat. I'm so happy you're home." Hard not to hug him again, lean into him, adore and admire him, and just soak up as much Crew awesomeness as I could in the few seconds I had before the kitchen timer went off.

Even when I tried to free him so he could do whatever it was that dinging sound insisted he attend to right away, Crew took a few extra seconds to cup my face in his big, warm hands, staring down into my eyes with his beautiful blue eyes full of love and affection, and kiss me, soft, sweet, light but full of passion despite the slow and delicate touch of those lips.

Hmmm. Maybe dinner could wait.

Crew left me to silence the siren call of supper, and I followed him into the kitchen, accepting the cold brew he fetched for me from the fridge. I sat while he puttered, knowing if I tried to help him he'd shoo me out of adorable frustration, preferring to do the cooking while I sat and waited for his next masterpiece. He wasn't Mom, don't get me wrong, but he could whip up a meal that left me hunting down leftovers before bedtime.

Good thing I took up running again.

"I thought you were out of town until morning." So lovely to see him, to have him here. I never, ever complained that he was away two or three nights a week. And I never would. We both had what we wanted—not just each other, but the jobs of our dreams (not going there right now) and the freedom to do what made us happy—and if his joy was fed by following Dad's lead and chasing cases outside Vermont, I was all for it. He'd spent so many years with the FBI, wearing a suit, following the rules, and then as sheriff of Reading, being tortured by townsfolk still yearning for the Fleming touch of my very own father—how Crew survived everyone comparing him to my dad I had no idea—that having this chance to take cases that thrilled and excited him, choosing opportunities for his own satisfaction and monetary gain was my priority. I could handle sleeping alone if I knew he was happy.

"Liz didn't need me and I missed my gorgeous wife." Crew winked at me, grinning, ladling a heaping helping of lasagna onto his own plate before shoveling a smaller portion onto mine. Bless him, I'd only had to mention once I didn't have the capacity he did, and he'd adjusted accordingly. Actually speaking up and asking for what I wanted seemed to work with him, kept both of us smiling, loving each other, with not a single thing to complain about.

Who knew being direct was the key to matrimonial bliss?

"Congratulations, by the way," he said, carrying both plates to the small dining room table, leaving me to transport our beers and the basket of bread he'd sliced. He'd already set the space, settling my plate next to my napkin and cutlery, butter softening on the table with the fat little salt and pepper shakers. I settled into my seat with a sigh of contentment and sniffed the lasagna, rich aroma driving off all thought. "I hear you solved not one, but two, cases since I left two days ago." He shook his dark head, the short haircut he sported a time or two grown out to the thick and collar-length delicious waves I preferred. "I'm so proud of you."

I shrugged, smile winning before I could downplay his praise. "Small beans," I said. "But still fun." And that made me sigh all over again because I really needed to tell him what was going on. At least I was in a great headspace now and wouldn't just heart dump on him like a crazy woman. Thinking about the candy store save and the second case—helping Stevie Dunlop locate her son's stolen bicycle, "borrowed" by the neighbor's bully—I couldn't help but struggle with a sense of doom that rose at the thought of having to, yet again, find something else to do that wasn't investigating.

Crew set aside his fork before he even took his first bite, expression soft but grim, blue eyes worried. "Fee," he said. "Babe, what's wrong?"

I held it together as I told him what happened, proud of myself in turn I remained level and steady, didn't waver or freak out. In fact, as I finished filling him in on the phone call, I realized I wasn't on the verge of losing my crap anymore. Maybe I was learning to deal with my emotional responses to things. Besides, everything had an answer. And I got to sit here, with the most amazing man I'd ever met, in the town that I loved, surrounded by people who cared about me, doing a job I'd been born to do. And no one, not even some petty bureaucrat with the name Lance (who did that to their kid?) could take that away from me.

We'd sort it out. From the frown on Crew's face, the way he'd gone stiff and grim, I knew if Lance did show up in town, he'd better watch himself. Emile might have been protective of Daisy, but Crew? I'd almost died on him a few times, so his level of safeguarding my person sometimes went a bit over the top.

When he spoke, though, there was no indication

he planned to harm the guy in any way in the soft tone of his voice. "We'll take care of it," he said, sounding so confident I smiled back at him. "Have you called your dad?"

I shook my head, fork toying with the cooling pasta on my plate. I'd lost my appetite despite my attitude. "I will," I said. "I just didn't want to dump it on anyone. I'm sure it'll be okay."

Crew's eyebrows arched. "Who are you," he said, "and what have you done with my wife?"

Smartypants husband creature.

I couldn't resist Crew's dinner for long, devouring most of what he gave me and two slices of bread before groaning my way into the kitchen to clean up. Though it wasn't a rule or anything, I took it on myself to make sure I tidied after he cooked. I was better at this part anyway, and by the time I'd finished loading the dishwasher and wiping down the counter, he was sitting on the sofa with his feet up, fresh beer happily accepted, fat pug half-lying across his lap while I snuggled next to him and settled my head on his shoulder, only partially paying attention to the news broadcast on the TV.

I took a second to leave Dad a message when he didn't answer, short and to the point, hoping he got it before the morning so he could back me up when the board inspector arrived. Trying not to worry, knowing my father would never let me down, I chose to put aside my anxiety for the remainder of the evening and focus on being with Crew.

A movie followed, early bed shortly after,

Petunia's nighttime walk quickly accomplished. I realized as I ushered her inside, pajama cuffs damp from the dew on the grass she'd dragged me into, I'd become half of a boring married couple, and I couldn't be happier about it.

Our lives were generally exciting enough. A bit of couch and dramedy distraction was exactly the sort of evening that I'd always dreamed of. As delighted as I was for Daisy? Times like this, having my happily ever after? Worth everything I'd gone through.

And no one would ever take it away from me.

Crew was up early, on the road, sweet kiss goodbye for me and Petunia perking me up as much as the scent of fresh coffee coming from the kitchen.

"Good luck today," he said. "You got this."

Right. I had a job this weekend. I almost let the call yesterday shake me enough I forgot. Well, I'd just do my best and carry on and we'd see, wouldn't we?

We certainly would.

I took my time getting ready that Friday morning, sunlight streaming into the living room while my pug crunched her way through her breakfast, slurping up the extra strawberries from my toast and peanut butter, nabbing my go-cup for a refill at Sammy's on my way to the office. I felt funny in my suit, though the gift from Liz had been a welcome offering since I had never owned a suit in my life and always admired how she carried herself in hers. While I was by no means FBI issue, suited or not, I at least could make myself look the part for my clients.

It was a gorgeous day, not a cloud in the deep

25

blue sky, towering mountains keeping the breeze at bay, the warmth reminiscent of summer but without the overpowering heat that sent me running for AC. I enjoyed my stroll downtown, Petunia huffing happily beside me, pausing a time or two to wave at neighbors who wanted a chance to greet the darling pug everyone adored, to share a bit of gossip and even a giggle or two, before carrying on toward work and my life.

Lance who? There was no way anything could possibly go wrong today.

No. Way. Wait. What?

No. Way. It couldn't be.

I froze in my tracks, go-cup forgotten in my hand, Petunia whining softly when she came to an abrupt stop at the end of her short lead, looking back at me with giant eyes filled with accusation I should have warned her already. None of which really registered while I stared in shock and growing horror at the sight of the tallish man with dark hair and a heavy, 70s mustache, potbelly protruding over his jeans under his plaid button-up, who quickly passed Sammy's and turned the corner, disappearing from view.

It wasn't until he was gone I realized I'd forgotten how to breathe and gasped a sharp inhale, hands trembling, body reacting with a wave of dizziness that almost sent me to my knees. I gasped a little, panting for air, free hand on my knee as I bent in half and caught my breath. Weird to have such a reaction to the sight of someone who couldn't possibly have been who I thought he was because the person I was sure I didn't just see was locked up. For trying to kill me. Okay, holding a gun on me. Betraying me to the Pattersons. Spent his whole life hating me.

I must have mistaken the man on the street. A tourist, likely. Some visitor who simply resembled the last person in the world who should have been walking the byways of Reading.

Because my most hated of cousins, former sheriff's deputy turned convicted criminal, Robert Carlisle, was safely ensconced in prison.

CHAPTER FOUR

I SKIPPED SAMMY'S, DESPITE Petunia's protests at not only missing out on her morning donut hole but the rapid pace I urged her into and went right to the office. Toby wasn't in, leaving me to unlock the door, slip inside to the chime of the welcoming bell, turn and slam it shut behind me, leaning against the glass, and finally stopping to contemplate the fact that I was losing my mind and I really needed to get a grip already.

Someone knocked on the door and I squeaked in protest, spinning to come face-to-glass-to-face with a rather plain-looking young man on the other side. Despite the warmth of the day, he was dressed in an overcoat over a suit and tie, his receding hairline carefully combed to disguise the fact though the bright sunlight clearly showed the shine of his scalp underneath. Hazel eyes, rather deeply set, wrinkled at the corners as he frowned and pointed at me, then at the door.

Whoops. I pulled it open, stepping back, pretty sure I knew who this was though we hadn't met, even as he extended one hand and shook mine with a limp and rather damp squeeze that lasted only long enough to tell me he would rather not touch me at all.

The feeling was mutual.

"Ms. Fleming," he said, and I recognized his voice immediately. "I'm Lance Dustin with the Vermont Board of Private Investigative and Security Services." He'd already told me that when he called, he didn't have to repeat himself. Then again, maybe he liked the sound of his own voice since he went on again, already scanning the office and noting, I knew, the fact I was alone, not even our receptionist there as a filler. "It's 9:05AM, Ms. Fleming. I said 9AM sharp." Was that a sneer as he brushed past me and moved further into the office, down the narrow space toward the end and Dad's desk? He paused next to mine, glancing at the stack of files, turning slowly to meet my gaze. "Where is your supervisor?"

I'd stepped forward as Lance helped himself to the office, so when the door chimed behind me I jumped yet again. I half expected Dad or Crew to rescue me, almost disappointed when I realized it was Toby arriving. She didn't hesitate at the sight of our visitor, placing her purse under her desk before smiling at me in that professional way of hers.

"Can I make coffee?" She took my go-cup from me and headed to the back of the room and the coffee maker, nodding to the inspector on the way by, though she didn't bother introducing herself.

Bless her, she might not have been my immediate salvation, but she gave me the breathing room I needed to gather my thoughts and pull myself together. Where was Dad? I'd forgotten in my brief and horrified moment of mistaken identity (it had to be mistaken identity, had to be) Lance was making his appearance this morning.

Maybe part of me wanted to forget, too. But there was nothing I could do about it now, and with my father absent—where was he?—I was left holding the squirming feline fighting to escape the confines of its bag.

"Dad's out for the morning," I said, hoping I didn't sound desperate, nodding to Toby who was on her way back to the front of the room and, once past Lance, gestured secretly at me she'd gotten the message. I pointed to the chair on the other side of my desk, inviting Lance to sit, but he didn't, instead looking around with that expression of distaste on his face, as though he'd smelled something that didn't agree with him. "I'm sure I can clear up any questions you have, Mr. Dustin."

"Well, I'm not so sure," he said. Wow, grumpy much? "From what I'm seeing here, one of the issues appears to be valid. You need a supervisor with you at all times, Ms. Fleming, during your sixty days. You knew that when you applied. So where, I ask you again, is your supervisor? Being out for the morning is unacceptable."

Okay, so this was how things were going to go. Did he really want to fire up the old Fleming redhead temper? Because if he wanted me to lose it on him, I was all for it.

Knowing, even as sparks set off in my head and a fire lit itself in my stomach, this was the worst possible way I could go about tackling the problem and the best possible way to lead me to be banned from becoming a PI for the rest of my life.

I could hear Toby on the phone, knew she had to be talking to Dad. Problem was, Dad was out of town, too. Despite my phone call last night, he must not have been able to make it home in time. Why hadn't I followed up? I kicked myself even as my mind raced over possibilities. How close was he? Could he get here in time to save me from ruining my future before it even got started? I struggled for a reply to Lance's demanding questions, not sure what to say that wouldn't make things worse, when Toby hung up and quickly joined us.

"Coffee's ready," she said. "Mr. Dustin? How do you take yours?"

"I don't drink coffee," he said, proving to me then and there he was a monster and there was something epically wrong with him and if he talked to Toby like that again I was going to make sure something truly awful happened to him and no one would ever find his body.

Toby, on the other hand, merely smiled and turned to me. "Cream and sugar, Ms. Fleming?"

I nodded, loving her so much at that moment, the way she diffused me and handled him with that simple acknowledgment that I was her boss, and this was my place and he'd be well served to show some freaking respect.

"I'd like to know a few things before I answer any questions," I said, instantly feeling more confident when his shocked surprise at my strong comeback took him off guard. Right. Bullies didn't take being challenged very well and if I could gain the upper hand, there was a good chance I could eliminate this threat to my happiness without resorting to, well.

Eliminating this threat to my happiness.

Lance shook off the surprise my response created, crossing his arms over his chest, a rather ridiculous look since it wrinkled the front of his slightly-too-large overcoat and made his particularly skinny body look like a kid dressed in his father's clothes. "There have been concerns raised, not only about your application and the proper procedures being followed to satisfy the sixty-day process but also about your ability to follow through in this job." I know I was frowning, inhaling to respond, when he went on, talking over my ability to protest apparently his favorite thing ever. "I can't grant your license until everything is addressed and my concerns satisfied."

"You mean the concerns of the board," I said, a little more dryly than I'd intended, while Toby snorted her amused agreement as she returned and handed me my coffee at the exact perfect moment to make him look like a total and utter idiot.

And I'd been worried about this guy? Seriously. Pathetic.

I sometimes had this terrible problem with underestimating those who held my life in their hands, and had, several times, almost died because of it. This time, though, my reaction felt accurate, despite the fact I knew he could ruin me if he wanted to.

Just try it, mister.

"Fine," I said, not bothering to wait for him to correct himself because tit for tat, I'm not above you, "we'll address those. But I deserve to know who is accusing me of misconduct and why they think I won't make a good investigator." I had an excellent track record, thanks. Thirteen—make that fourteen, fifteen, oh, wait, *sixteen*—bodies and counting. Yes, I'd made a few enemies along the way, so it was possible one of them had decided since I'd made their lives miserable, they owed me. I just hoped my years of being a busybody hadn't ended in my sabotaging myself on the cusp of having what I wanted all along.

Lance didn't answer, the door chiming behind me interrupting our conversation. I turned, hoping it was Dad, knowing it wasn't when I heard Toby gasp out loud in response to whoever it was that walked over the threshold.

The world settled into slow motion while I

finished my spin, that same blow to the gut I'd felt earlier, the inability to breathe, the vague sense of panic and powerful surge of denial stopping my heart for a beat or two, freezing me in place and making it impossible for me to do anything but wait as Robert Carlisle closed the distance, smirk as familiar as ever, the disgusting caterpillar of dark hair over his upper lip revolting in its lurking weight, potbelly thrust outward toward me while his jutting jaw and thumbs hooked in his belt loops completed the horror show.

"Hello, Fanny," he said. "Aren't you happy to see me?"

CHAPTER FIVE

IT TOOK ME A moment to realize it really was him and that, in fact, he wasn't an apparition, made up by my already unbalanced brain or perhaps a projection, a hologram from some sci-fi movie. Or that, naturally, he wasn't alone, his ever-faithful girlfriend and bane to my existence—and poor Daisy, whose status as her half-sister gave me no end of the heebies—Rose Norton, lingered behind him in her khaki deputy's shirt that was decidedly too big for her uber-skinny frame. Wow, I thought Lance looked like he was a kid in daddy's clothes. Rose was thinner than ever, and that giant work shirt made her seem skeletal.

"Rob." Lance extended his hand, shaking Robert's returned one, telling me exactly why the inspector was here and who had complained and that I was never, ever getting my PI license, was I? Not while my should-be-incarcerated cousin and his clearly delighted bonesfriend (girl, eat a hamburger) entertained themselves by making my life miserable.

"Lance," Robert said with that oily smile that turned my stomach, "I wanted you to meet my fiancé," his, choke, gross, "Deputy Rose Norton." Another handshake and I hoped his palm was as moist for them as it had been for me. "Thank you for coming with such haste. As you can see," my cousin looked around with so much obvious judgment it was a clear caricature of the buffoon he really was, "my concerns about Ms. Fleming's supervision weren't unfounded." When had he learned to speak like a pompous ass?

Maybe they taught it in prison. Regardless, he was singing Lance's song, the inspector nodding, grim and accepting of one side of this particular story. Seriously, he hadn't even given me the benefit of the doubt from moment one.

Ahem. So, I'm sure you're acutely aware of the fact that a) Robert was right and I wasn't supervised and b) no, I didn't have two years' experience aside from my less-than-professional busybody nosiness, and c) likely everything Robert claimed had some basis in truth so the fact remained I really, probably, most assuredly wasn't going to become a PI after all.

Didn't make me feel any better or less willing to argue the points, however.

Turned out, I didn't have to. Because about one

second after I drew a heated breath to counter the pair of them, Rose clearly enjoying the spectacle as she stared at me with a hateful smile and beady eyes, the door opened one more time, the merry chime of the entry bell precursor to my salvation.

All in the form of the tall, broad-shouldered and now mostly-silver-haired ex-sheriff even Robert was afraid of. My father's easy smile and deep-seated self-confidence radiated out of him, silencing Robert, shutting down Rose's smirking grimace, and catching the attention of Lance Dustin who cleared his throat as though suddenly uncomfortable and rather embarrassed to be there.

Well now. Did he and Dad have some history I wasn't aware of?

"Lance, good to see you." Apparently so. Dad reached out, clapped the slim young man on the shoulder, not even sparing Robert a glance, though he had to be as shocked as I was that my cousin was on the loose, right? My hopes perhaps he'd broken out of prison, and I could arrest his sorry ass died in the face of my father's calm handling of the next few moments. "Hope Montpelier is treating you well. Missed having you on the department when you left."

So, Lance had been a deputy here? Huh. Then what was his freaking problem?

Right. He'd been a deputy with my cousin. Lovely.

"I called Lance in," Robert said, puffing out his narrow chest while Dad continued to pretend that not only was his nephew not present, but no one had spoken.

"I heard you were working for the PI Board." Dad chuckled. "Nice change, I assume, from being in uniform?" Yikes, I couldn't tell if that was a jab or a genuine question. With Dad, sometimes? It was hard to tell.

Lance didn't seem to take offense, however, though he did stiffen up and resume his rather tart expression and tone of voice. "I'm here to do my job, Sheriff Fleming," he said, before blanching and shaking his head. "I mean, John. Mr. Fleming." He stuttered through that while Dad just smiled at him, big hands on his hips, looking down at Lance with patience and kindness and grown-up charisma while his former deputy floundered.

I'd have been enjoying the show if it weren't for Robert's scowl, Rose's snarl. They had plans and there was no way even Dad could stand against them, I was sure of it. While this attack—oh, make no mistake, this was a full-out battle in what was likely to turn into a war to end all wars—might not succeed, I had zero doubt that if my cousin was on the loose on purpose, it was with purpose.

The question remained—what idiot let him out of prison and why?

"Of course you are, Lance, my boy." Dad nodded, smiled. "Wouldn't have it any other way. I understand you have questions about Fee's qualifications? My supervision?"

Lance glanced at Robert whose sullen expression

must have told the inspector he'd lost any advantage he might have felt he had dealing only with me. "I do have a shortlist," he said.

"Excellent," Dad said, clasping his hands together before rubbing them vigorously, visibly unphased by the reveal. "Fee and I have a job today, so unfortunately we don't have the time to chat, but we can make an appointment." He spun while Lance fish lipped, clearly wanting to protest. "Toby, can we make Lance here an appointment?"

"Of course, Mr. Fleming," she said with that perky smile of hers. "Mr. Dustin?"

Instead of succumbing to Dad's suggestion, Lance seemed to crumple slightly, shaking his head, hands stuffed now into the pockets of his overcoat. "I'll be by again," he mumbled. "Where are you working so I can observe?"

"White Valley Lodge," Dad said. "Private security for a convention. You're welcome to come and check things out." My father grinned. "It's going to be one of those long and boring weekends."

I wished Dad hadn't said anything as I watched the wheels turning in Robert's head. Then again, it wasn't exactly a secret where we'd be or who hired us, so it was likely my cousin and his girlfriend were going to show up at some point and make themselves a pain in my neck anyway. Besides, Rose must have known. Sheriff Jill Wagner was responsible for part of the security, the lodge's staff the rest, Fleming Investigations hired separately for an extra layer of protection for the convention's participants. Though what a group of small-time inventors needed with so much security I had no idea.

"I see." Lance hesitated, awkward and liberated of all the bully-like energy and strategy he'd tried to pull on me. "I'll be seeing you there, then." He hurried out, nodding to Robert who followed after, miming tipping his hat to Dad, to me, Rose trailing along behind him.

My father watched them go with that same small, careful smile until the door shut on the backside of trouble at which point he exhaled heavily, one big hand sliding over his face.

"That was close." He grinned at me like it was funny. "You okay, kiddo?"

I was going to kill him, and no one would hold it against me when they found out why. "Tell me you didn't know Robert was on the loose."

Dad shrugged, clearly uncomfortable himself. "I just found out," he said, voice low and tense at last. Shook his head, shoulders drooping enough that towering John Flemingness I was so used to—and took such strength from—was gone for a moment. Dad had this presence to him, this sense of mountainous eternity and endless invulnerability I envied and wished I could emulate. But every once in a while he let his guard down in front of me and it always made me as worried as it did grateful he was willing to be himself, his real self, even if it was rare and the times far between.

"Is he really out, John?" Toby joined us, looking

up at Dad through her glasses, overhead lights shining on the surface enough to block her eyes. But her thin, pursed lips and the way she clasped her hands in front of her Fleming Investigations fleece vest told me she was as worried as Dad should have been.

"He is." My father shrugged then, tossed his hands, confidence returning while he gusted a loud and crisp sigh. "Nothing we can do about it. Or Lance. At least, for now." He poked a finger at me. "I'm just glad I was close by. I was heading back to town anyway after getting your call last night. Why didn't you let me know right away?"

How did he know…? Toby, right. She must have guessed my nutso reaction to the call I received before I left was tied to this.

"Sorry, Dad," I said. "I wasn't in any kind of mood to talk to you after he called."

Dad nodded. "Well, I have some time, so let's get you set up at the lodge." He glanced at his watch with a little frown. "Toby, can you call the client and tell them I'll be along?"

"No, Dad," I said. "You go. Lance won't be by this morning." Dad cocked an eyebrow. "And even if he shows up, the lodge is big. I'll send him on a wild goose chase. Will you be far?"

"Just in Killurn," he said, the slightly larger town a mountain over. Maybe a forty-five-minute drive. "I can be back pretty fast if he gives you trouble."

"Perfect." It wasn't like the small jobs I was taking paid our bills. Dad and Crew, and sometimes

Liz while she exited the FBI, were the real moneymakers. I had no illusions they were just keeping me busy here until I had a license, could take on the bigger stuff with them. No way was I holding anyone back when there were alternatives.

Dad thought about it a moment then shrugged. "Okay, let's do that," he said. "Don't hesitate to call." He hugged me quickly, kissed my cheek. "You got this, kid. You're already a better investigator than Lance or Robert will ever be. Let them try to stop you."

I smiled, nodded, shoulders back, Fleming at the ready. "Good luck, Dad," I said.

Watched him go with a sinking feeling in my stomach I'd made a terrible mistake but unwilling to call him back. He was right. I had this. And I could stall with the best of them.

With a wave for Toby, I got Petunia moving, to-go cup still filled with hot coffee and heart in my throat and headed out to do my job.

CHAPTER SIX

I DROPPED PETUNIA OFF at The Iris, as usual, though I couldn't help stopping to talk to Mom this time, despite knowing I was the bearer of bad news she didn't need to hear but would likely stumble over and preferred she heard it from me and not some gossiping neighbor.

She didn't take Robert's freedom very well, cursing in a rather unladylike fashion at the news, though she did retire to the privacy of the kitchen from the main foyer to do so.

"Fee, this is ridiculous." She was actually huffing, redheaded temper showing up rarely despite our matching hair color. She must have thought this warranted an outward release of her unhappiness and I couldn't have agreed more. "How can he be out?

He was just convicted."

"Something happened, obviously," I said, feeling oddly better having Mom to talk to. Dad hadn't been much help but she, at least, knew how to express anger in tandem.

She hugged me, took Petunia's leash, the pug already begging for snacks with soft huffs of breath. "Let me see what I can find out," she said. "You go to work, sweetheart, and trust your father, please. He knows what he's doing, and he'd never put your business at risk." She was right. Then again, Dad did have a rather blasé of a way about him lately, since stepping down as sheriff, as a matter of fact. "Don't let that horrible young man give you a hard time." Yes, I let her in on Lance and the license issue, of course, I did, though whether she was referring to him or to Robert I had no idea.

Then again, she'd never refer to my cousin as a young man—harsher language was called for in mention of that particular not-quite-a-human being.

The lodge looked beautiful in summer, though I missed the heavy layer of snow that gave it that winter wonderland feel skiers seemed to prefer. I loved the lush, green lawns and the endless trails through the evergreens, the mountain hikes and the new path leading to the *Zip It!* zipline park a few miles away. Jared's friend, Carmen Martinez, had sold it to Emile when the mogul came calling, so everything was now all grouped together in one big amusement park for the outdoors inclined. I personally loved ziplining, though I did have a rather unpleasant memory tied to that activity. Still, I'd managed to shut that history off to the side in favor of recalling how fun it had been to swing through the trees with my beloved Crew.

I strode up the front steps to the main entry, passing through into air-conditioned comfort and an interior that felt far more wintery than the outside scape. Tall, white walls, towering glass features and cascading crystal chandeliers gave the lobby of the lodge a sense of walking into a frozen, ultra-modern movie set, the wide counter welcoming guests, marble floors shining underfoot, piped-in music soft and unobtrusive.

I wondered if Emile was going to make changes or keep the décor? Didn't matter to me, though I did love the way the lodge looked. Alicia Conway—now Conway-Wilkins, I reminded myself—and Jared's new wife of only a year, had a big hand in assisting with the design, back when she worked for Jared's father, Pete. While the elder Wilkins might not have been the most honest—or nice, or friendly, or human—person on the planet, he had made the right decision including Alicia in the interior decorating. Sure, he'd skimped on the building materials that kept the place structurally sound to the point it took over a year after he was gone to make things right again, but the surface stuff? He'd outdone himself.

Speak of the devil, I spotted the beautiful blonde behind the counter, her dark suit and white shell making her look way more professional than I did despite Liz's gift, partially because she wore it like she meant it and I felt like an impostor still. I kicked myself for judging—it was only a matter of habit and comfort I'd soon get used to—and promised myself I'd own this look as I joined Alicia at the counter.

She hurried around to hug me, one-hundred-watt smile as big as Jared's had been. "Fee," she breathed my name, "I'm so happy you're here to take charge of security." She eye rolled at me, huffing out a little laugh of frustrated amusement. "If I have one more question about if the inventions are safe, I'm going to strangle someone."

I grinned at her, shrugged. "Fleming Investigations to the rescue."

"Fee." Sheriff Jill Wagner stopped next to me, nodding to Alicia who nodded back. "Is John coming?"

I shook my head, hoping it wasn't a mistake to do so. Would she tell Lance if he asked? "Tell me you didn't know about Robert." Way to throw out a distraction and some gossip at the same time.

Jill flinched, grimaced. "I only now found out." So, same pipeline as Mom or what? "He just showed up," she said, sounding stunned, cheeks pinking. "Any idea what happened?"

Alicia gaped at us both. "He's out?" She shivered, rubbing both arms with her opposite hands. "I need to call Jared."

I let her go, turning fully to Jill. The tall sheriff's pale eyes were as troubled as I'm sure mine were, her dirty-blonde ponytail shivering as she sighed, hooking both thumbs in her gun belt. Robert had made it look obscene, but Jill Wagner? Unlike me and my suit, yeah, she owned this look and always would.

"I'll find out what happened," she said. "I hear there's trouble?"

I glanced over her shoulder, hoping talking about it wouldn't summon the demon. "Nothing I can't handle," I said, not wanting her to have to worry about my status. She'd been on the other side of me poking my nose in where it wasn't wanted long enough. Jill didn't have the easiest job in Reading and landing more problems in her lap wasn't my plan for the day. "I'm here for my client," I said, switching to professional mode. She took the hint, straightening and gesturing for me to precede her toward the ballroom doors.

"I'll introduce you to Doris Campster," she said. "She's the one who hired you, I think?"

"Dad handled it," I said. Froze in my tracks, choking on the need to explode even as a familiar face appeared at the double doors, Rose beside him. "Why is he here?"

Jill scowled at Robert who waved back, grinning. "I don't know," she muttered, "but he won't be here long."

Before she could flex her sheriff's muscles and eject him, Robert handed her a business card the instant we stopped in front of him and his deputy girlfriend. Of course, his big, gross smile wasn't for the sheriff but me while Jill stared down at the printing on the white rectangle for so long I finally broke eye contact first to lean in to see what it said.

And choked for the second time. Carlisle Investigators, Private Investigation and Security, Robert Carlisle. Phone number, email address, and that was that.

"Since when?" Jill looked up, clearly at a loss for anything else to say. Hey, she was way ahead of me. I couldn't even put two words together let alone speak at all.

He shrugged, sniffed so his mustache crawled in disgusting ripples. "I took the training years ago," he said like it was no big deal he was infringing on Dad and Crew and me and, damn it, no way. No. *Way.* "Before I became a deputy. Had my license since forever." He flicked his fingers at me. "Before your dad." Meaning, he wasn't the one following footsteps.

Asshat.

I didn't get to kick him or take Jill's gun and shoot him or even say something clever and witty or snarky and cutting. Instead, I had to suck all of that up as a smallish woman with a round face and equally round glasses, her dull, brown hair in a tight bun at the base of her neck pulling her skin a bit too tight for comfort, joined us, hands clasping the front of her brown cardigan to her like she needed the protection.

"Sheriff Wagner, I hope there's not going to be any trouble." She had an unfortunate voice that wasn't quite annoying but came close enough, her pinched and anxious eyes going back and forth between Jill and Robert. "Meanwhile, I'm still waiting for the private security I hired." She peered at me through those glasses, wrinkling her nose so the pads climbed up the bridge and settled the frames more firmly against her bushy eyebrows. "Unless this is her?"

I held out my hand, cutting off Robert who already had a card extended. "Fiona Fleming," I said. "Fleming Investigations. It's a pleasure to finally meet you, Ms. Campster."

She leaned left to look around me, face contracting into something resembling a weathered apple. "I understood there was a gentleman with you. John, I believe?"

"My father is already looking around," I said, hating that I lied so easily but knowing if I didn't, if Robert knew I was here alone, Lance would be bringing license Armageddon down on me before I could spit. Jill didn't look shocked at my temerity, so she must have decided staying silent was the best option, bless her. "He asked me to meet with you and coordinate your needs."

That was professional enough, right? She seemed satisfied, or, at least, sighed and shrugged her narrow shoulders over wide hips that made her roundness all the more pronounced. "Very well," she said. "This way, please, Ms. Fleming." She frowned at Robert who still had his card out. "We're not open to the public until Sunday," she said, before turning her back on him and walking away.

I didn't laugh out loud, but came very, very close.

We didn't make it far before the intensely focused form of our town mayor hustled into our presence and put an end to forward motion with the sheer force of her will tucked tidily into her pale cream suit. Olivia Walker's penchant for shiny black bobs did little to update her style, though she always looked the part of powerhouse leader.

"Doris!" She firmly shook the woman's hand between both of hers, smile widely politico as she spun on me with that hungry look in her brown eyes I recognized instantly as Olivia at her very best—or worst, depending on what side of her you fell on. "Fiona, how lovely. I heard you and John were hired to assist." She spun back to Doris who stuttered in surprise at the overwhelm that was our mayor while I bit back a giggle. I was used to Olivia. Doris was not. "Excellent choice, by the way. You won't be disappointed." Another look, this one severe. "Will she, Fiona?"

Ah, a threat from the mayor. My day wasn't complete without a threat from the mayor.

"Fleming Investigations has things well in hand," I said. "If you'll excuse us, Olivia, Doris was just giving me the tour." I gently took the older woman's arm in my hand and guided her away before the mayor could stop us, Doris blinking up at me in shock.

"She's rather aggressive," she finally muttered.

"She loves Reading and is delighted you're here," I said, realizing if I did, in fact, lose my opportunity to become a PI, I could hire on with the mayor's office as damage control and a spin doctor.

Yeah. No. Thanks, though.

"I have to speak to our guest of honor." Doris relieved herself of my grip, blinking up at me from her less than five-foot height. "Tour the facility—I'm certain you're familiar with it already—then give me a report when you're done." She cleared her throat, adjusting her glasses with one hand. "I've been accused of being lacking in my care of security in the past, Ms. Fleming. I don't want any incidents at this convention. Do I make myself clear?" She hustled herself off in a rolling walk that covered ground faster than she should have been able to at such a height while I inhaled slowly and promised myself I could handle this.

CHAPTER SEVEN

JILL SAVED ME FROM being too overwhelmed about being on my own, rejoining me shortly after Doris made her exit. I had stepped back out of the central space and through a gap between two displays, telling myself it was a good vantage point while knowing, ultimately, it was more about having a moment to catch my breath. Our town sheriff seemed to get it, didn't comment on my slightly trembling hands or the fact I was practically hiding out rather than doing the job I'd been hired to do.

"It'll be nice to see John," she said, all casual. Plausible deniability reinforced? Check. Except, of course, Alicia would have to be alerted to the deception to make the lie complete. Regardless, Jill didn't seem to judge me for my lying ways. Nope, that was my job. I muttered something that satisfied her because she chuckled and squeezed my shoulder with a knowing look. "I never thought I'd see the confident-to-a-fault Fiona Fleming as pale as a ghost and not a body in sight."

That made me grin, giggle a little, though honestly there was nothing funny about death or corpses, but she knew just the right tone to use and I needed the release of laughter to shake off my stress.

"Jill," I whispered, "I have no idea what I'm doing."

"Fee," she whispered back, "welcome to the club." And then she laughed, and I laughed with her and, sadly, that was the truth of the state of affairs in our dear, darling little town. Really instilled confidence in me, I'll tell you.

Didn't matter, though. The moment of warm camaraderie was more than enough to still my trembling, get my heart beating in a more natural rhythm, all while giving me the time I needed to remind myself what I'd been asked to do wasn't life-altering or rocket science.

Look around. Pay attention. How hard could it be?

"John's not coming at all then?" Jill waved off my intake of breath, my regretful expression, grinning. "You don't need him," she said. "I'd have you as one of my deputies in a heartbeat. You used to be my sheriff, remember?" She winked. "And you're the reason I have this cushy job in the first place." Was that wry regret behind her joking? She'd wanted to be sheriff for as long as I knew her, had stuck things out, had Crew's back, even tolerated working with Robert and Rose for the chance to have this job.

Then again, I could hardly blame her if she decided it was a terrible idea. Being sheriff in Reading amounted to kowtowing to Olivia and her gang of tourism-centric bullies while tolerating small-town gossip, judgment and switching sides when it came to support and/or criticism of every single move she made, personal or otherwise.

"You're welcome," I said. "If I can help, Jill, let me know."

She shrugged, lips twisting into a grim little smile. "Now that you're a PI, maybe you can investigate why Matt hasn't proposed yet."

Oh. Boy.

I could tell by the instantaneous shift in her body position, in the tension that gripped her shoulders, the flat and unhappy expression that overwhelmed her face, she regretted speaking that little tidbit out loud. I didn't get to ask any questions or commiserate or even hug her as she nodded abruptly to me and headed out, her tall, broad-shouldered self far more sheriff than pining girlfriend.

Matt Winston needed his very handsome park ranger butt kicked. He and Jill had been dating for a couple of years, far longer than Crew and myself. I'd only been peripherally aware of the fact they'd failed to follow through on getting engaged after they'd moved in together. Yes, because I was a crappy friend with a lot on her plate. No excuses, honest.

Now that I thought about it, the two had seemed tense in each other's company the last few times we'd gone out to dinner or to play pool, though I'd brushed their attitude off as that familiar gruffness some couples adopted. Considering both of them were in law enforcement and weren't exactly poster kids for expressing emotion, it wasn't all that hard to create a story around the pair of them that they simply decided not to go further and were happy/unhappy as they were.

But now? Jill had triggered my friend radar and if Matt Winston thought he could get away with having his very attractive cake without lighting her candles? He had another thing coming.

Because poking my nose into the personal lives of my friends? They had to know that came part and parcel with my adoration.

Not that I was about to march off and do war with the ranger or anything, but he was damned lucky a heated conversation caught my attention and distracted me from the irritated thoughts I was thinking. Two women had repeated my retreat and invaded the space behind the displays, heads down and together, whispering in hissing anger that made it obvious whatever they discussed was likely going to devolve into an all-out fight if I didn't intervene. Mind you, it was clear from their appearance they were mother and daughter, the younger a slimmer and slightly taller cookie-cutter of her parent, with the same dark hair in high ponytails, identical cheekbones and jawlines and, as I approached, the same pale green eyes.

The older of the two cleared her throat, taking a step back while her daughter crossed her arms over her chest, scowling in that angsty teenage way at the floor that made me think of me and what a bratty redhead I'd been when I was her age. I nodded pleasantly to the two of them, the mom offering me a flash of a smile that never reached her eyes, gaze flickering to her daughter and back to me again.

"Can we help you?" She unconsciously smoothed her hands down the front of her blue and white striped button-up, tucked neatly into navy dress pants, black belt capped with a regular buckle, black pumps and tiny silver earrings her only conventions to womanhood. Her daughter, on the other hand, in her slouching jeans, hoodie tied at her waist and 80s punk band t-shirt clearly put little effort into her style and look, perhaps part of the problem.

"Fiona Fleming." I handed the mother a card and, in passing, one to the daughter. "Fleming Investigations. I'm here as private security for the event."

The teen sighed and looked away, but the mother seemed happier to find me there. "Thank goodness Doris finally stepped up," she said, shaking my hand. "I'm Nicole Powell and this is my daughter, Callie." I offered to shake with the girl, but she just backed away another step. Friendly. "There's been no end to problems at previous events with strangers allowed to walk through the displays under little to no supervision and free access to other people's projects without permission."

Callie sighed again, this time the exaggerated expression of an irritated teenager. "It's not that bad, Mom." She eye rolled at me. "You're so paranoid."

A tall, attractive man poked his head through the gap, taking note of the two and then me. He joined us, offering to shake which I did, noting the way he seemed to hover, protective of the pair.

"Teddy Kring," he said.

"Fiona Fleming." Another of my cards changed hands.

Teddy glanced at it, graying hair buzzed short still thick, long, lean frame relaxed but as casually uncaring of style as Nicole's if his khakis and sneakers topped with a generic golf shirt were any indication. "These two giving you trouble?" He half laughed, going for a joke, and I let him have it, smiling in return while the teenager released another of her impressive exhales.

"Not at all," I said. "Just making my rounds, introducing myself."

"Delighted," Nicole said. "Now maybe I can actually trust my invention will be safe from people trying to steal it."

Callie made a face at her mother, eyes flat. "Just stop, Mom," she said. "No one wants to steal your stuff. They all have their own."

"Not all of them," Nicole said. Her daughter opened her mouth like she was going to argue and, instead, turned and left, skirting the displays and continuing down the back end until she disappeared at the far left.

"You have to forgive the girls," Teddy said. "Mothers and daughters don't always make the best invention partners."

Nicole shrugged up at him. "If only she'd take an interest." She seemed saddened by that, offering me a little smile. "She used to love coming to these events with me. Callie is so bright. I just know if she applied herself…"

Wow, did my parents say the same about me?

Teddy, meanwhile, squeezed her shoulder and, in that moment, I had an epiphany. While it was clear to me they weren't together—Nicole was just too distant with her body language for them to be dating—it was obvious from his sad and watchful expression he wished things were different.

Huh. I really was getting good at paying attention.

CHAPTER EIGHT

"MAY I ASK WHAT you invented?" It seemed a reasonable request for me to make and, it turned out, was the best question to distract Nicole from her retreating teenager. She beamed at me then, leading me out through the two displays toward her space. Hers was a large, dark blue concave construct of cardboard curved inward like a semi-circle with giant clouds and lightning crossing the surface. *Lightning In A Bottle* titled the top of the display, a writeup with her bio picture beneath it talking more about her invention though Nicole was already reaching for the glass jar with the metal turntable inside.

"We're in crisis, as an entire world," she said, "looking for inexpensive energy alternatives that can replace fossil fuels." Tell me something I didn't know. She flipped a switch, and the turntable began to spin, humming softly while the glass jar lit up with a faint glow. "My invention generates electricity through magnetism but without heat as a byproduct."

"They're doing it large-scale with trains and other vehicles," Teddy said, sounding excited, "but to have small, portable energy generation, safe enough for personal use but powerful enough to run someone's home? That's revolutionary."

Okay, he was obviously impressed so I was, too. "How does it work?" That was me, nosy despite the fact I was pretty sure even if she did explain it to me I'd never really understand. It was hard not to ask, though, in the face of their enthusiasm.

Nicole hesitated before turning off the machine, visibly deciding to keep the ins and outs to herself. "It's hard to explain to the layman," she said, though it was clear she wasn't being totally honest as to why she wouldn't go into more depth. Callie had been right. Her mother *was* paranoid. And fair enough if there had been problems in the past, though whether imagined or not. Doris's decision to hire me, on the other hand, created enough momentum for Nicole's concern I brushed off her rejection.

Teddy seemed embarrassed by her reticence and smiled at me while I smiled back so they'd both know my feelings weren't that easily hurt. "I'm an engineer," he said, "and even I don't fully understand it." Yeah, that sounded weak to me too, Tedster.

Nice try, but thanks for playing.

Nicole's faint answering smile told me I'd likely outstayed my welcome no matter my willingness to accept her excuses or not.

"Thank you for the demonstration," I said. "I hope this weekend is productive." I left them before things could become even more awkward and sighed to myself, hoping everyone I met at this little convention wasn't so protective of their work it made them rather unfriendly. It wasn't like they had anything to fear from me. I had a career, thanks.

Well, hopefully.

Nope, not going there right now.

I didn't make it far, chatter from the gathering getting louder as I stepped away from Nicole's display and toward the center of the empty ballroom. They'd set up a stage in the middle, though no one stood there just yet, the crowd surrounding someone who suddenly broke through, wide, Hollywood smile as fake as his highlighted hair color, ruggedly handsome enough if you were into the slightly overweight, beginning to decline athletic type who was so used to being the center of attention he didn't know how not to seize focus and do anything to keep it. I held off from the flow of people now following him as he began a slow tour of the space, not stopping anywhere in particular, his gaze instead seeming to float over everyone and everything as if nothing caught his attention or was worth his while.

Yes, I knew his kind and was not impressed.

Oh, he knew how to smile and wave, don't get

me wrong, how to play the gathering, his movie-star act fooling everyone, it seemed, but me. I almost laughed out loud at his booming voice, the way he paused for dramatic effect when he spoke, deciding to follow and observe while he deigned to grace the rest of us little people with his presence.

I had no idea who he was until he paused, tall and overly skinny woman in a crisp suit at his side almost clinging to him—wife or girlfriend?—and I paused, unable to help the disdain that had to be written all over my face.

"So, you're not a fan of Blake Hughes, I take it?" I turned, startled, to face the man beside me who watched the unfolding drama with his own tight grin of judgment. Shortish, about my height of 5'7", shaved bald but with the head shape to carry it off, he winked one hazel eye at me, thin lips twisting further, hands in the front pockets of his jeans, dark dress jacket over his fitted t-shirt at least professional/casual. "But he's a superstar, you didn't know that?"

I snorted, shook my head.

He seemed delighted to have an audience. "The man's a poser," he growled softly, though still amused, if dark and rather grim, "and that wife of his? Isobel?" He clucked his tongue. "Piece of *work*."

"So you're not a fan either then," I said.

He laughed at that, grinning with real humor. "How'd you guess?" My companion watched Blake carry on but made no effort to follow and I chose to remain and gain the insights he shared. "He hasn't had a solid invention in at least a decade. But everyone says he's a genius, that he's brilliant. Whatever." He rolled his wide shoulders as though attempting to shed the weight of Blake Hughes's ego. And, maybe, his own? Because it took a pompous ass at times to know one, right? I reserved my opinion as my companion went on. "I can't believe Doris brought him here to keynote and teach. And judge the competition on Sunday. You ask me, he's washed up and needs to step aside for someone else to shine."

"Like you?" I arched an eyebrow at him, knowing that sounded judgy but pretty sure that was the best tact to take and reassured I'd read him right when he barked a laugh.

"*Moi*? Not likely." He fished into his jacket, handed me a plain, black card with white writing. Gavin Baker, consultant. "I don't create the inventions. I just help inventors get their work out there into the world."

Hmmm. "You consult with them on next steps?" Interesting job.

He nodded. "Help them navigate treacherous waters," he said. "Apply for patents, avoid scams, legal advice, manage them if they want, find funding. That kind of stuff."

I hadn't noticed that Blake's entourage had turned, that the man himself had headed back our way and was almost on top of us while Gavin filled me in. It wasn't until I heard that booming voice say my companion's name—okay, shout it with anger behind it—that I switched focus back to the star of the show in surprise at his clear animosity.

Because while Gavin had been derisive, Blake appeared livid.

CHAPTER NINE

"WHAT IS HE DOING here?" Blake jabbed an index finger in Gavin's direction, the woman my companion identified as the star inventor's wife, Isobel, looking down her narrow nose, though without the same level of clear disgust her husband managed. "This man is an affront to all inventors, and I demand he be removed at once!"

Okay then.

Doris appeared through the gaping gathering of inventors and their support staff, looking about as harried as she had when we'd first met, though rather than side with her guest of honor, she instead stood between the two men with a grim and determined expression.

"Mr. Baker has every right to be here," she said. "As a paying sponsor of our event, his support means we can follow through with our convention, Mr. Hughes."

"This is an *outrage*." No, tell us how you really feel, Blake. His towering dislike wasn't moving Doris, despite his clear attempt to bully her into compliance.

"Mr. Baker's participation was outlined in the contract," Doris said. "I'm sorry if you disagree with my choices, but this convention is my responsibility, and I will do everything I can to ensure its success."

Wow. So, I was a little thin on the respect side of the scale for her initially, but now? She had my full attention and support. I took a half step forward, placing myself right beside her, another body between Blake Hughes and Gavin Baker.

I have no idea if my move actually helped or not, but Blake chose to back down, sullen expression telling me he wasn't accustomed to being thwarted, having his own way par for his particular private course.

"I'll have to seriously reconsider my participation, then," he said, spluttering faintly as though he wasn't sure if his threat was going to be sufficient.

"That would be a relief for everyone," Gavin said, from the tone of his own words enjoying this spectacle far more than he probably should have been. "Give my regards to obscurity and heyday on your way to the bottom of the barrel, won't you?"

Ouch. Though, kudos because he certainly had a way with insults.

Blake stormed off, Isobel in his wake calling his name, the crowd clearly unhappy with the unfolding drama. Before I could turn and address Gavin, ask him what the problem was—since he'd already told me why he didn't like Blake but had offered zero reasons why the feeling would be mutual—a tall, beautiful woman in what appeared to be her early fifties, bobbed auburn hair framing a face preserved with ample products and likely specialized services only available in a clinic, confronted Doris. She towered over the small woman, like most people in the room, though the frumpy older of the pair seemed far less in need of any kind of posturing to bolster her position while the slim woman in the expensive-looking gray skirt suit and spike heels clearly fought tooth and nail for her looks and her self-confidence.

"Elise Steel," Gavin said to me in a normal tone of voice but clearly not addressing anyone but myself. Like a play-by-play at a sporting event, he offered up background info. "Lawyer to the poor and desperate."

She ignored him, focusing on the event coordinator. "You can't be serious, Doris." Her deep voice vibrated with real concern as she glanced sideways at Gavin. My companion simply smiled at her, waved like this was the best joke ever and he was the only one with the punchline. "We've talked about this in the past. You can't allow this man to prey on others."

Interesting. I shot Gavin a questioning glance and

accepted his amused shrug and one-handed wobble of might be accurate, might be lies while Doris's response echoed her confrontation with her star inventor.

"I don't see you upping your sponsorship dollars, Elise," the older woman clipped in a crisp and accusatory tone that made me fight a grin at her chutzpah. "Gavin has every right to be here. And that's my final word on the matter. Now, if you'll excuse me, I have final setup to supervise."

Doris made no move to leave, however, waiting for the other to depart first. Elise shot Gavin a grim and unhappy look. "Keep your nose clean," she said. "I'm happy to represent pro bono anyone you rip off with your scam." Gavin didn't respond, seemed rather comfortable with such accusations, to be honest, for someone who was legit. Elise hesitated, likely expecting some kind of response she didn't get, before stalking away on those impressively high heels I'd have broken an ankle trying to navigate.

"People are so touchy," Gavin laughed. Winked at me. "I didn't get your name."

I handed him a card in return, and he chuckled when he read it.

"Guess I'll be keeping an eye on you, Mr. Baker," I said.

"Happy to have such beautiful eyes on me, Ms. Fleming," he replied with a twinkle in his gaze. "Looking forward to getting to know you better while you check me out." His utter disregard for anything resembling authority or concern had me on the fence as he waved and strolled away in the rolling gate of a short man with bowed legs while I tried to decide if he was charmingly harmless or a danger to everyone around him.

If the last few minutes were any indication, I'd be dealing with Mr. Baker and his class act before the weekend was over.

Doris drew close, frowning, lips in a puckered circle of unhappiness. "I need things to go smoothly," she said. "Can you handle that, Ms. Fleming?"

Right, because it was my job to make sure no one killed each other. Hoping that stupid joke that crossed my mind wasn't prophetic, I nodded with what I assumed was a sufficient amount of certainty because Doris huffed at me before moving off, leaving me with the dread-filled realization I'd taken on way more than I'd bargained for.

It was clear I had my hands full this weekend. Fortunately, however, the rest of the afternoon and evening spent on duty ended quietly enough, any further angsty confrontations either happening outside my purview or not at all, leaving me to observe, as promised, while the night shift of the lodge's security closed up shop and stood outside the ballroom doors on watch while I left to retrieve my pug and go home.

When I returned the next morning, alone yet again and a bit more nervous today, the first full day of the convention, Petunia happily ensconced at The Iris with Mom, I did so a half hour before my 8AM call time, taking the extra thirty minutes to tour the ballroom set up without anyone there, familiarizing myself with a space I already knew very well, knowing I was being overly cautious but wanting not only for Dad and Crew to be proud of the job I did but to make sure the client was happy.

This was my first major job for someone not from Reading and I had to make a good impression.

Doris arrived shortly before the doors opened and seemed surprised to find me there, the flicker of respect I caught crossing her face and the rather relieved way she greeted me gratifying.

"Busy day ahead, Ms. Fleming," she said. "I appreciate your punctuality." She peered past me into the room now filling slowly with inventors and their friends and family. Today and tomorrow were only for those involved in the convention, Sunday's open house for the public's edification making me sweat just thinking about security. "Mr. Fleming is out and about?"

"We have things well in hand," I said, getting very good at lying.

"I'm not anticipating trouble," Doris said, wringing her hands, "but things have been known to happen. Just stay on alert and I'm sure everything will be fine." Was she talking to me or herself? Didn't matter because she was already hustling off and I had a job to do.

I spent an hour doing my best to ignore the keynote speech Blake Hughes boomed through the speakers from his place on stage shortly after 9AM.

Fortunately, I had an excuse not to sit and watch, got to at least pretend I couldn't hear him pontificate. Sure, he probably had some great advice, but his delivery was nothing to write home about and I honestly chose to just block him out after the first five minutes.

Once he was done, a lineup of other inventors got up to speak, filling the morning with information, including the lawyer, Elise Steel, sharing her expertise in patent application. I waited for Gavin Baker to take a turn, but he never did, and though many of the inventors gathered seemed to openly avoid him, a few stopped to chat and he clearly turned on the charm because his table was rarely empty of someone to talk to.

While he might have been a con artist, he appeared to have game.

I slipped away for a quick bowl of soup in the kitchen, grateful that Alicia nabbed me and ensured I was fed. My feet weren't entirely happy with me, my choice of a low heel not the worst option but taking its toll, though I was able to ignore the aching for the most part in favor of interest in watching the inventors demo their inventions for each other. Some were clever—the self-chopping salad bowl would have been a great toy for my kitchen if it didn't malfunction halfway through a head of lettuce and spray the contents on those of us observing— while some were ridiculous—who really needed a machine to tie your shoelaces?—and others downright out there—a wearable alarm that shocked you awake if you didn't respond to it in time? No thanks.

While not entirely quiet—I had to come between two inventors who accused one another of stealing ideas and had to admit their inventions looked very similar—stop a suddenly depressed man from smashing his creation and wrangle a pair of teenagers who were messing with someone's display, sending them packing, giggling, off to their parents, for the most part it was rather boring and I was grateful for the intervening moments of something to do to keep me going so I didn't lose my mind.

Who knew being a PI could be so freaking dull?

Sure, everything I'd investigated before this had been tied to murder, missing pirate treasure, mysterious disappearances, clues left behind to lead me to truths exposing those who meant my town no good. I'd lived on the edge of excitement with each case, not realizing, I admit, that most of what a real detective did was grunt work, patience and, at times, failure.

No, I wasn't complaining. This was what I wanted. Still, having a few fires to put out—especially easy ones that barely started smoking before I arrived to stomp them into ash—gave me the forward motion I needed to make it to the afternoon.

Of the first freaking day.

Kill me now.

I nabbed Deputy Kit Somersby, Jill's newest recruit, on my way by the main doors about 3PM. She grinned at me, barely five-foot stature more than petite, her gun belt almost bigger than she was, black hair tidy in a bun at the base of her collar, deep brown eyes huge in her pale face.

"Bathroom break," I said. "Mind covering?"

Kit nodded. "Sure thing, Fee. Pretty quiet out there anyway." She sounded happy about that. "Take your time. I got you."

At least one of Jill's deputies was nice. I still couldn't understand why she hadn't fired Rose yet, though. Hadn't been lost on me, however, having an all-female sheriff's department was likely a bit of a novelty, so maybe Olivia was hoping to use that as a recruitment factor or some kind of tourism drive I had, as yet, to hear about and would probably be offended by in some way.

Not my problem. Besides, I had my own unfolding, I realized, as I entered the bathroom off the lobby to the sound of two women's voices shrieking in the tiled space, so loudly I couldn't make out the words.

CHAPTER TEN

IT WASN'T HARD TO head off the argument because the moment I set foot in the bathroom the two women backed off one another as though embarrassed to be caught by a stranger in such heated conversation. Nicole Powell could do little about the bright pink of her cheeks and the slight bulging of her eyes, though Doris seemed to recover instantly, likely accustomed to such interactions thanks to her position.

"Perhaps next time you'd like to take your chat outside and away from the public?" This was a bathroom open to all guests of the lodge, after all. "Is there something I can do to assist?"

"Yes," Nicole snapped, "you can eject that piece of garbage, Gavin Baker, from this convention."

"I've already informed you," Doris cut in before I could say a thing, "he's a paying sponsor." She tsked before her face settled into a truly grumpy frown. "You know, Nicole, I've been doing this job, creating this opportunity, for all of you for almost a decade now and what do I have to show for it?" She tossed her hands in the air, her voice rising in volume, her face flushing at last as her temper seemed to get the better of her. "Certainly not a single thank you or any kind of gratitude. Only complaints." Wait, was Doris on the verge of tears? I took a half step toward her, empathy in full force and annoyance with Nicole and everyone else involved growing by the moment. I'd been a bed and breakfast owner, understood the lack of positive feedback, the endless negative reviews about my darling pug and her flatulence, criticisms layered over any hint of positive and squashing out the last bit of life from even the most thinly veiled attempt at anything to do with increasing confidence and self-esteem.

Nicole's expression had softened somewhat, though that changed as Doris went on.

"Your personal issues with anyone I choose to include in this convention aren't my problem," she snapped then, tears visibly retreating. I now worried Doris might pop something vital as her face turned that purply color that seemed like a precursor to a stroke or aneurism rupture. "Perhaps if you were more discerning about who you slept with, I wouldn't have to listen to your complaints." Doris pushed past me and out the door, stomping footsteps audible even after she exited the bathroom and that was impressive considering the heavy door swung shut behind her.

As for Nicole, she trembled with her own anger renewed, hands clutching at her opposite elbows as she hugged herself, barely contained inside that personal embrace.

Well now. Seemed like information was easily acquired in this particular subgroup. Good to know just in case I had to ask questions and get answers to uncomfortable queries.

"This has nothing to do with Gavin and me." It seemed very important to Nicole I understand that. Her tone of voice instantly dropped as a pair of adorable twentysomethings—clearly dressed for a hike—giggled their way into the bathroom and a pair of stalls. Nicole's whole body shifted, shedding her tension visibly though it was acutely obvious she still held it inside, if barely, as she sidled up to me, whispering the rest of her story. "Yes, we had a relationship, but it was years ago, just after Callie was born. I haven't had anything to do with him since I realized he isn't in this business to help inventors but take advantage of them." She scowled at the door and Doris's absence. "She's right, though. We don't thank her enough." Nicole sagged a little while the girls emerged and washed their hands, staying silent until they left. From the understanding looks they shot me they were well aware something was unfolding though they didn't need details.

No, they didn't. But I did. "Do you have proof

Gavin isn't legit, Nicole? Because sponsor or not, I can talk to Sheriff Wagner."

She shook her head, a few strands of her thin, dark hair escaping her ponytail to trail down the side of her neck. "There's nothing anyone can do," she said. "I've heard from countless new inventors who have used his services." She almost spit that word at me. "None of them have been successful with either criminal or civil cases against him. He knows what he's doing and how to protect himself while draining them dry."

So, he did everything legally. Which meant there wasn't anything I could do to help.

"Just steer clear of him," I said, "and do your best to forget he's here. Unfortunately, he's not going anywhere."

Nicole's lips pinched together but she nodded then. "I'm usually better at keeping my temper," she said. Yeah, I told myself that same lie, too. "Just, do me a favor?" I heard the door swish while someone entered, Nicole's intense gaze locked on me and keeping me from looking to see who it was. "Keep an eye on Gavin? One of these times he'll make a mistake and he'll finally pay for what he's doing."

I didn't get to promise her, because she brushed past me and was gone, though when I looked up and realized Elise Steel had been listening, I wondered at the faintly cynical smile she shot at the retreating Nicole.

Not for long, the patent lawyer shrugging at me, elegant self perched on those precarious heels.

"Gavin again?" She snorted a laugh. "You do know they have a history?"

"I'm aware," I said.

"It's a small community." Elise strode to the sink, shoes clicking on the tile floor. She washed her hands as she went on, checking her makeup in the mirror as she did. "Everyone has a history with everyone, Ms. Fleming, and passions run high at times." Good to know. Her gaze met mine through the mirror when she shook the water from her hands, helping herself to far more paper towels than were necessary in my opinion, but I'd been a small business owner and paper towels? They were expensive, yo.

"Does that include you, Ms. Steel?" I hadn't meant to challenge her, but her whole attitude had my back up and I really, really needed this job to go well.

Elise just smiled, turning to face me. "Naturally." She sighed then, crossing her arms over her chest with the grace of a ballet dancer performing a rehearsed move. "I've had my indiscretions. Nothing meaningful, mind you, but still. A bit of advice?"

"I'm always open to advice." Why did I want to just smack that condescending smile off her face? Instead, I dove deep into Dad and pulled out cool confidence.

Elise shrugged like she knew I wasn't listening but figured she'd share anyway. "Any attempt by an outsider to correct old wrongs will only gain you grief or, worse, get you fired." She laughed at that. "We're happy in the little hell we've made for ourselves. Just put out the small fires and leave the rest of what you uncover to the continuing drama that is this gathering of wannabe inventors, thieves, liars, cheats and con artists."

"Again," I said, "are you included in that roll call, Ms. Steel?"

Elise didn't comment, simply walked past me and out into the foyer, leaving me to ponder what she said. Because despite myself, the insider information actually was welcome. Now that I understood the dynamics of what was going on—no different, really, than the inner workings of my very own Reading and the populace more than happy to wind out their own dramas without anyone interfering, thank you—it was easier to relax into the job.

If something did go wrong? I'd deal with it, though it sounded like, barring something absolutely catastrophic, as long as I did what was asked of me, things would work out just fine.

That whole thing about renewing my confidence and feeling good about myself and what I was doing? Seemed doomed to take hits, no matter how hard I tried to the contrary. Because the moment I set foot in the lobby, shoulders back, head high, ready to get back in there and make Dad and Crew proud, Lance Dustin appeared through a small crowd of guests lingering in his way.

"Ms. Fleming." He was practically shaking as he stopped next to me, closing the distance between us in a long stride of one seized by passion. "I thought I made it clear to you. You're not permitted to perform duties as a private investigator during the course of my investigation." He said *what* now? While I fought off the panic that took over while I tried to figure out what to say to that, he made matters worse. Head whipping from side to side, he then refocused on me, expression settling into base bully. "And where," he said in a low voice vibrating with self-righteousness, "is your supervisor?"

CHAPTER ELEVEN

WOULDN'T YOU KNOW, DORIS chose that exact moment to join us? Heard the whole kit and kaboodle too, if the deepening scowl of suspicion on her face was any indication.

"Ms. Fleming," she said. "What is the meaning of this? I hired you to do a job. Are you incapable of doing that job? And where is your father?"

Another person looking around for someone who wasn't there. Awesome.

The very best (sarcasm, I swear) part? Robert appeared as if from nowhere—though clearly from nearby where he lurked like a bloated spider ready to suck the life from my soul and take everything that meant anything to me before crushing me into the ground—with a business card outstretched to Doris and a disgusting smile wriggling the furry pet on his upper lip.

"Robert Carlisle, Ms. Campster," he said. "Might I suggest a change in agencies? There are a number of complaints against Fleming Investigations under ongoing scrutiny while my agency is ready and willing to take over."

She actually reached for the card while my whole world crashed down around me.

There were times when Olivia Walker was the biggest pain in my rear I'd ever experienced. Times when her annoying insistence on micro-managing Reading into the kind of place she insisted it become created enough tension I was positive I'd lose it. And instances when I could only laugh and shake my head and wish her the best, knowing she was, at least, doing her best and that she'd brought a level of prosperity to the cutest town in America no one else would ever be able to manage.

But only once in a while, when the timing was perfect, and the circumstances aligned with the Universe and my impending doom did Olivia Walker step up and become my hero. The first time had been the day I'd been accused of murder. The handful of others I consigned to history.

Today? Today was one of those days.

"Mr. Carlisle," she said, shouldering her way between him and Doris, "has just been released from prison and is hardly a good choice for this event." He spluttered while Doris dropped his card as if it bit her. "Now, either you trust in me and my office, Ms. Campster," she said, no longer the over-eager and ingratiating mayor I had come to know but commanding, demanding and powerful, dominating the conversation and literally locking out anyone else's opinion with the sheer weight of her presence, "or you can pack up your little convention and leave my town. Today."

Wow. Just. Freaking. Olivia. My *shero*.

Doris, clearly flustered, shook her head. "We're already set up and open," she said.

"Precisely." Olivia's smile was back, arm around Doris's shoulders. Wasn't lost on me Robert crouched to retrieve his fallen card. Just how I wanted him, kneeling at my feet. Roar. "Ms. Fleming has special dispensation from the town of Reading to carry out business inside our municipality. You can check the paperwork at town hall if you so choose, Mr. Dustin." So, she'd had a run-in with Lance already, had she? He'd made himself a nuisance if her cold manner meant anything. "And of course, she's being supervised, though why a woman with such an incredible crime-solving track record requires supervision I have no idea." I could see Doris's confidence in me returning with every word, her own shoulders rounding back as she nodded to me, though Olivia wasn't done. "I just saw John Fleming outside touring the property. And your own dear Crew Turner," she nodded to me, "was talking with Alicia, I believe, about the parking lot lighting."

She might have been lying and she might have

been telling the truth, but either way, it was impossible to tell. While I'd been learning the ropes, Olivia Walker was a master and I almost bowed to her, fighting off the grin of gratitude and surge of internal emotion that rose from her stalwart support. Of course, I knew she was serving her own interests and that if I ever tried to thank her she'd firmly and crisply tell me if I screwed up like this again she'd make sure I paid for it. But, in that instance, she had my back, and I would not let her down.

Lance's scowl told me he didn't believe her, though it turned out it didn't matter. Because Dad chose that moment to enter the main doors, stride toward us with his easy smile, clasp Lance on the shoulder while he nodded to Olivia—was that a flicker of relief in her eyes?—before holding out his hand to Doris.

I almost missed the fact Crew was with him, Dad made such an entrance. My husband frowned at Lance before giving me one of those sly and sexy smiles of his, big hands tucked in the front pockets of his denims, dress shirt buttoned not quite high enough to hide the curve of his collarbone beneath.

Yum.

Fee. For pity's sake. Focus.

Lance seemed utterly shocked to find them both there and, from the look he shot at Robert, his source had let him down. My cousin backed off a few steps, glaring at Dad, while my father continued to ignore his nephew and carry on business as usual.

"I hope this kerfuffle isn't our fault." So innocent

and so fake. You know, I'd spent my whole life admiring my father, seeing him as a pillar of justice and truth and all that was good and right in the world, even when I was mad at him. To discover, these last few years, he was just as willing to deceive, bend the rules and make things happen in ways that probably didn't exactly fit the standards I'd set for him had been a bit of a blow to my daughter ego.

The fact my amazing father wasn't perfect, however? Was my problem, not his.

"Not at all, Mr. Fleming." Doris put a final end to the matter, nodding to Dad, to Crew. "Delighted to meet you in person. And to have all three of you here, well. Our little convention is honored." She seemed flustered by the fact. Likely had spent the last ten years, as she'd said to Nicole, fighting for everything she'd accomplished, including being taken seriously.

Dad had just given her the biggest gift and likely cemented himself as Man Of Doris's Year. So John Fleming of him.

"Our pleasure, Ms. Campster," Dad said, gesturing toward the ballroom. "We need a few minutes to confer if you don't mind. All three of us have a few suggestions we'd like to see enforced now that the convention is in full swing, and we've had time for an on-the-spot assessment."

"Of course," Doris said, blinking behind her glasses. "I appreciate any feedback."

"Hopefully it's all information you can use to your benefit at your next event," Dad said with that charming Fleming smile and rugged good looks. Big hero moments much, Dad? "If you'll excuse us, I'll track you down in a half-hour or so?"

Doris bobbed a nod. "Thank you, Mr. Fleming. And Mayor Walker. I'm so glad we came to Reading this year."

Olivia beamed at her, her turn to drape a friendly arm around Doris's shoulder. "And every year," she said, leading the woman away.

While I stood, stunned by what I'd just witnessed, impressed and rather anxious about Dad's ability to manipulate people—I'd never seen him use his powers so blatantly before and didn't know if he'd done so for good or for evil and wasn't sure I wanted to know—he spun on Lance with a shift in personality so rapid and complete I worried about the inspector for a second.

"If I knew what your problem was," Dad said at his most coldly disappointed, "I might have some understanding of just what it is you intended with this little display, Lance. But I don't know, and I honestly don't care. The fact remains your attack on my daughter, whether you believe it was founded or not, is an affront to me, to our business and this profession. If an honest and talented investigator can't conduct herself with permission while following the rules without being continually harassed in the course of her duties, I'm beginning to wonder if the board's mandate serves anyone, let alone the people of Vermont."

Okay, so the second time today I was floored and

amazed. And while Olivia only occasionally filled the bill of my shero, Dad's continuing fluctuations from a human being with flaws to SuperDad had me a little breathless.

Lance spluttered. Lance tried to make excuses while shooting surreptitious glances at Robert. And, knowing he was beaten and clearly not happy about it, Lance backed off.

"Ms. Fleming," he turned toward me, pale as a sheet with two very bright pink points at the tips of his cheekbones, not meeting my eyes, "I'll have a ruling for you first thing Monday morning. Good luck with your event." With that, he spun on his heel and marched toward the doors, Robert pausing a moment, looking like he wanted to say something, before hurrying after his friend.

"That kid," Dad said with a sigh. "I had high hopes for him. Never understood why he let Robert get to him. It's the reason I had to let him go."

"I thought he liked you," I said. Wow, that sounded whiny.

Dad shrugged, voice low and only for the three of us. "He liked Robert more, kiddo." He glanced back over his shoulder one more time, Crew and I already watching as Robert caught Lance just before he reached the doors and the two, silhouetted by the sunlight outside, left together, heads down.

"This could still be a problem, then?" Crew didn't sound worried, but I knew him better than that.

Dad just sighed. "I have a friend on the board. I'll give him a call, see what's going on. If there is trouble, it's not really about Fee. It's about me. And I'd like to know who might be targeting us if this is bigger than Robert."

Wait, why would Dad think that? Unless he'd already been having problems he didn't tell us about. Because that would be all John Fleming, all the time.

I didn't get to ask him anything, though. Dad leaned in and kissed my cheek, grin back in place. He'd always been so stoic when I was growing up, when he wore the uniform of sheriff of Reading. He'd softened a lot since he'd first retired then gone private, but he still knew how to hide his true feelings from me.

"You two have fun now," he said. "I'll see you in the morning."

"Wait, he's leaving?" I turned to my husband. "I thought…" Paused and sighed. "You, too?"

"I," my amazing and gorgeous and delicious husband said, guiding me toward the ballroom, "need a tour of the facility, please, and a shortlist of things we can bring to Doris Campster to fulfill your father's side of the bargain."

Because Dad hadn't had anything to say, made that up, too.

Disillusionment, thy name is daughter.

CHAPTER TWELVE

DON'T GET ME WRONG. I was delighted to have Crew with me. We so rarely got to work together. Still, as the rest of the day wound down, I couldn't help but feel pathetic that I needed my husband to babysit me. That was, after all, what it amounted to. And yes, my pride was rather interwoven with my feelings of self-worth at the moment, so sue me.

It didn't help I was also experiencing a surge of ineffectuality as the afternoon turned to early evening and the proceedings wrapped up with no further fanfare. Yes, I understand the difference between wanting things to be more exciting and having to deal with the imminent possible loss of my ability to do my job or even finding a dead body or uncovering some massive conspiracy that would lead to the end of the world. And no, I wasn't asking for anything ginormous or earth-shattering or even overly dramatic. Boredom, however, had seeped into any vestige of confidence I'd managed to salvage and tuck away for a rainy day and devoured my will.

Sheesh, Fee. Get a grip already.

I made the mistake, as we locked up for the night, Rose the attending deputy this time who smirked at me and Crew and bossed around the lodge staff like a savage, of asking my husband if the job was always this dull.

He had to laugh at me, right? Make things worse? "Trust me," he said, "boring is preferable to the alternative."

Lucky he'd done that laughing before he climbed into his new SUV and drove off instead of after when I could fume and take out my frustration on him unimpeded. Instead, I had the short drive down the mountain to pick up Petunia to defuse the ticking Fleming timebomb that was my irritation at his reaction so when I did walk through the doors of The Iris, Mom simply handed over my pug with a kiss on my cheek and a lovely, maternal smile instead of having to make up the guest room at her house so my husband wouldn't have to sleep on the couch. His house or not? You'd better believe he'd be the one not sharing our bed after a fight, you betcha.

It was clear to me when I finally reached home, Petunia panting her waddling way to Crew for a scratch and likely her hundredth snack of the day because she was obviously starving, the poor dear, I was the problem. Poor Crew shouldn't have had to bear the brunt of my frustration or put up with me losing my temper over things he didn't have any control to fix. While intellectually I understood this, it was still hard to hold back and I fear I was a little waspish with him that evening, apologizing so much he finally hugged me after a particularly snarky comeback he hadn't earned.

"It's going to be okay," he said.

"I'm sorry I'm being mean." Choke. Damned tears. Him hugging me wasn't helping. And was, at the same time.

"I've got broad shoulders," he said, "and more love for you than you can ever know. I can take it, Fee. I know it's not me."

Still wasn't right but that little talk actually helped. By the time we curled up in bed, Petunia between us, snoring herself into silly oblivion, I'd shed most of the worry that drove me to distraction and angst and was able to fall asleep myself without too much trouble. Best and most caring husband ever.

The phone ringing jarred me awake, Crew reaching for his cell, clock on the bedside clearly announcing in bright blue letters it was just past 2:11AM.

"Liz." Crew said her name by way of greeting, gruff voice thick with sleep. That shifted instantly as he sat up, the sound of her voice faint from the other end of the line, enough information being shared he tossed aside the covers, letting cold air in, darn it, and headed for the bathroom. I closed my eyes against the light that appeared under the door, groaning a little at being woken from a deep sleep, but knowing what a call this late meant.

Crew was buttoning his shirt when he joined me in the kitchen. I poured hot coffee into a travel mug for him, the perk barely making enough to fill it halfway by the time he was ready to go.

"I'm sorry," he said, kissing me slowly, cheek pressing into my hair when he hugged me. "This is important. I'll be back tomorrow, but if I don't go now, the whole case will fall apart. Liz needs backup and I'm closest." He rocked me a little. "This could mean big things for us, Fee. Giant."

"Just not anything you or Dad or Liz can tell me about." Apparently, I was still clinging to the crabbiness from earlier. Before he could protest, that hurt look on his face my punishment for speaking up when I knew better, I nodded. Chose the good wife routine over my previous nastiness, hugging him back. "Forget it, I understand. Just... Crew, is it anything I should worry about?" and shook my head against his chest. "Never mind. Just be safe."

He kissed me one more time. "I'm sorry I can't tell you more," he said. "I love you." And was gone out into the early morning. I locked the door behind him, returning to bed, only then realizing Petunia slept through his departure. That made me sad for some reason, though likely it had something to do with Crew leaving and my very bad day that I sat for about a half-hour and cried quietly into my hands until I fell asleep again.

Not to last, my phone's ringing this time waking me. Another look at the clock read 3:26AM. I'd barely gotten back to sleep, no wonder I felt so disoriented. I answered anyway, knowing I probably sounded groggy and not caring.

"Ms. Fleming." I knew the voice but couldn't place it, rubbing at my eyes and yawning as the woman went on. "This is Nicole Powell. From the convention?" I perked a little, though recalled instantly her own daughter called her paranoid and wondered if this job was worth it after all.

"What's wrong, Nicole?"

She sounded muffled, voice low like she was whispering, and I found it hard to make her out. "Can you please come to the lodge? I need to talk to you."

Wait, how did she get my number? Right, everyone had one of my cards. That was a dumb idea, Fee. "Nicole," I said, "if you're having trouble with security, you can contact the lodge's people who are there to guard the room for the night." No, I didn't suggest she talk to Rose Norton because, deputy badge or not, she was the last person I'd send anyone with a problem to.

"They won't listen to me," she hissed. "Please, I really need your help." She hesitated a moment before going on. "I think someone was trying to steal my invention."

Sigh. "I'm on my way." Because what else was I going to say?

CHAPTER THIRTEEN

THE DRIVE UP THE mountain cleared my head of a lot of things, not just my lingering sleepiness. In fact, by the time I reached the lodge, Petunia curled up in the front seat, snoring, I'd worked through enough of my self-doubt issues that I was actually happy Nicole called when I hefted my pug in my arms and carried her snorting self toward the front doors.

I had a job to do. This was the job I always wanted, at least, something in law enforcement. I refused to let anyone, or anything, sully it for me or make me doubt myself. Lance Dustin could try. Robert could, too. Some mysterious someone Dad seemed to think was out to get him could take their shot, go for it. But this was my dream and until I was told point-blank I couldn't work as PI ever again, I'd be fulfilling my obligations to my client.

And if we're going to be frank here, knowing my track record? Even after that.

Made me smile, even snicker a little, despite everything. I set Petunia down in the lobby and let her waddle her way forward, leash in hand, lighthearted and happy again. When had telling me not to do something ever worked out to other people's advantage? I'd be fine, Fleming Investigations would flourish and my life with Crew would turn out the way I'd hoped all along.

Nicole was waiting for me by the main doors to the ballroom, Rose scowling at her, then at me as I joined them. I chose Dad's tactic and ignored the deputy, smiling at Nicole like I had all of this in hand and wasn't fast asleep after crying myself into that state of unconsciousness from feeling sorry for myself.

"Tell me everything," I said. "I'm happy to help."

Rose inhaled like she had a lot to say about that, but Nicole's grateful hug interrupted the super-skinny deputy.

"Thank you," the inventor said. "No one else would listen and I'm at wit's end." She glanced at Rose who crossed her arms over her chest, head tilted to one side.

"Ms. Powell seems to think someone tried to rob her." Rose sounded bored, annoyed. "I assured her no one would want to steal from her." The tone of her voice was bitterly amused enough I knew she meant ill of the woman, like who would want to steal her trash. Luckily, Nicole didn't know Rose like I did and failed to pick up on the veiled insult, instead focusing on me.

"I came down to check on my booth," she said. "I forgot to make sure I had a second plug for the backup unit and wanted to be sure everything was ready for tomorrow." She wrinkled her nose. "Today." So, she understood she'd dragged me out of bed? Good for her. I nodded for her to go on and she did. "Someone was in there, Ms. Fleming. I saw them." Panic lit her eyes, bulging them slightly. "Near my booth."

"But not at your booth," Rose said, same tone, same attitude.

Nicole didn't answer her, mute and afraid.

"You do realize," Rose drawled, "you're not the only inventor allowed to go inside and check out her stuff, right?" She eye rolled at me then seemed to think better of trying to gain sympathy from my corner. "You're being paranoid." From the way Nicole flinched, she was very tired of hearing that term aimed in her direction. "So, you might want to just go upstairs and stop making trouble for the staff."

I wondered how deep a ditch I'd dig myself if I punched her in the face. Instead of finding out, I gave the next question the full weight of my displeasure.

"I need a list," I said, jaw jumping, "of everyone who went in and out of the ballroom since we shut down at 6PM." Rose was about to protest, written all over her, but I waved off her argument with a sharp cut of one hand. "Now, Deputy Norton. That was not a request."

"I don't work for you," she shot back.

"No, but you work for Reading and the mayor won't like to hear that one of her employees failed to fulfill her duties when asked to do so." So there, you little git. "The list, deputy. I don't have all morning."

It was obvious in the next ten minutes as Rose attempted to gather said list that communication between her and the staff of the lodge had broken down to barely tolerable levels. Rather than let Rose make a further mess, I took aside the head of security for the resort, Ross Mullen, and asked him personally while he shot hateful glances at the deputy.

"She's a horror to work with," the middle-aged security head said, his shorn silver hair shining in the light of the foyer, face red with anger. "Tell Sheriff Wagner I won't work with her again and neither will any of my people. I'll be filling Alicia in on everything, believe you me."

"I'm sorry, Ross," I said. "I know she's a handful. But right now, I need your help. Can you tell me who was in and out tonight?"

He seemed to take control of himself, nodding, professionalism kicking in. "Sorry, Fee," he said. "You and your dad and Crew always played straight with me, Jill, too. I was happy when I heard Robert was getting what he deserved. Is he really out?" He shook his head before going on. "Never mind, weasels always find a way to escape." Ross drew a final breath and settled. "As far as I know, according to my guys, there were quite a few in and out since we shut down." He glanced at a sheet of paper in his hand, some kind of sign-in page. "Gavin Baker," he said. "Claimed he forgot his phone at his booth, was in and out shortly after midnight." Too early to be Nicole's creeper. "Isobel Hughes. Said she left some personal papers with her husband's things at his booth." Blake's gaudy display was twice the size of everyone else's and promoted his single successful invention, a cooking tool I'd always imagined would break after one use. Sure, the flashy thing could do six different tasks, but it seemed rather over-the-top to need something that could grate, cut, chop, slice, dice, crush and whatever else it did or didn't do when classic tools seemed much more efficient.

Whatever, not my problem that people loved to buy junk they then hid in drawers in their kitchens and never used. The craze of his epic slicer/dicer had died out within six months of its arrival but made his name for him.

"She was here at 1AM?" Again, too early.

Ross checked the sheet he showed me. "Looks like it. She wasn't in there long, maybe ten minutes. Then, about 2:15, Doris Campster was here and toured the room. I was going to go with her but Deputy Norton wanted to do it and we had a bit of a disagreement." He grimaced like he hated the fact she got to him so much. "By the time I turned to escort Ms. Campster she was already inside, so I left her to it."

Not Nicole's suspect either. "Was anyone else in there when Nicole went to check on her power issue?"

Ross shook his head, again showing me the sheet, this time handing it off. "Her kid, Callie, was here, but that was a half-hour before Ms. Powell showed up." Interesting. "And that Kring guy, Teddy? He was around, too. But, again, they were both gone before Ms. Powell arrived. Right, that lawyer lady, Steel? She was here, earlier, though. Forgot her purse. As far as I know, the room was empty when Ms. Powell was in there." He glanced at Nicole before lowering his voice. "As much as I hate to agree with Deputy Norton, I have a feeling that woman's a bit on the nervous Nelly side if you know what I mean?"

I did, nodded my thanks, handing the sheet back. "I'll talk to Jill," I said. "This will be Rose's last shift with you. Okay?"

He sighed in clear relief. "It's not that I can't handle her," he said, "it's just she's a pain in the tuckus and my guys have their hands full with drunk guests and such. The deputies and you guys at Fleming Investigations are supposed to take this kind of stuff off our plate, not make more trouble."

"I get it," I said. "I wish I could help more. This is the best I can do for now."

"I appreciate it, Fee," he said, hand on my shoulder, clearly back in control of himself and actually smiling. "Remind your dad he owes me five bucks from cards on Sunday?"

Right, like I was his collection agency. "I'll handle Nicole," I said. "Just stay clear of Rose and enjoy the rest of your night."

Ross saluted and walked away, his black uniform reminding me a little too much of the professional soldiers I'd had recent run-ins with. Reminders of the past aside, I had my own work to do and rejoined Nicole as she watched with wide eyes and a growing expression of doubt.

"I was alone, wasn't I?" She shook her head, misery crawling across her face. "I'm sorry. I was so sure."

"Let's make sure," I said, one hand on her elbow, guiding her to the ballroom door and the dark interior. "You and me. Okay?"

She nodded, clearly grateful, and I spent the next few minutes touring the quiet, dim interior. There were emergency lights on far overhead, but nothing that would illuminate the space to the point of real clarity. I could see, as I strode toward Nicole's display, how things could look scary in the dark, though I wasn't going to tell her that.

Instead, once we'd finished our tour and she checked the plug situation she wanted to inspect—assured her invention was safe and sound and present and accounted for—I sent her up to her room, waving off her quiet thanks for coming and for listening and headed for the back room behind the front desk.

One of the staff looked up when I knocked, smiling, her dark brown hair tied neatly behind her white collar, dark suit the preference for desk staff.

"I need a peek at your surveillance footage from the ballroom," I said, because better safe than sorry.

The girl wrinkled her nose, shook her head, but was up and moving, heading for the computer and bank of monitors. "I'm happy to help, Ms. Fleming," she said, her silver nametag identifying her as Crystal, "but the camera system has been glitchy lately. Lots of static. We have a tech coming in from the manufacturer but..." she shrugged and queued up the ballroom footage.

Grunt. She wasn't kidding. There was more static than image and I quickly sighed and waved off any further attempt to find what Nicole might or might not have seen.

Since no harm was done, why did I bother? Because this was my job. And I loved it.

Mostly. There were times, when I was tired from being woken twice, after a day of trouble I hadn't been expecting, and crying myself into a stupor while worrying about my sweet and elderly pug that I really, really wondered what it was that I loved about being a busybody.

Like five seconds after I exited from behind the front desk and ran right into Blake Hughes.

CHAPTER FOURTEEN

I WAS SORT OF expecting him to give me flack, to maybe stir up trouble or prod me into some kind of argument about security. What I wasn't expecting was what happened next.

His smile had that oily edge to it that often preceded inappropriate looks and comments and, to his credit, he owned up to the expression brilliantly.

"I'd heard the head of security was a gorgeous redhead," Blake said, deepening his voice—I'd heard him speak earlier today at length, so it was very obvious he'd done so to try to impress me—and leaning in, eyes roving the front of my button-up under the dress jacket I'd thought to throw on over my jeans. "I'm not disappointed."

Just ew, dude. "I'm sure your wife is," I said,

speaking before I could stop myself because, as I was well aware, my lips and my brain often had miscommunications when it came to appropriate behavior in polite company. Then again, there was nothing polite about this piece of work, so I didn't feel so bad when he cleared his throat, a faint frown telling me I'd hit the mark.

Dead center.

You're welcome, Mr. Grossness.

"How delightful," he said, deadpan, before heading for the bar. Not his room, the elevators, but the twenty-four-hour gin joint. And *I* was delightful?

Petunia yawned one of her cat-like meows at me, seated rather ungracefully at my feet, looking up and blinking in slow motion while waiting for me to make up my mind.

"Fine," I told her. "Let's go home. Happy?"

She chuffed at me, licking her lips, clearly anticipating some kind of treat on the other end of our journey. Seriously, who made pugs so freaking food motivated? I'd love to meet them and shake their hand before kicking them somewhere very painful.

I did manage a couple more hours of sleep so when the alarm went off at 7AM—so blissful to have that extra hour I never got when running Petunia's— I wasn't as groggy as I expected. In fact, I was halfway through breakfast of toast and peanut butter—yes, my favorite—Petunia begging for scraps when the front door opened, and Crew returned.

While I might have gotten enough rest, he clearly

hadn't, yawning even as he bent to kiss me.

"Problem solved," he grinned, sinking down next to me and scratching Petunia's ears. "I'm glad I went. Liz wrapped things up, so we finally get our payday." He seemed super excited while I fought off my continuing frustration I hadn't been filled in on the case she'd been working on and felt rather put out by being excluded. Cut short when I took firm hold of my ego and shook it a little to make it smarten up.

Staff meeting pending, license, too. I'd get the details eventually, right? Besides, did Liz know everything about what I was doing? Dad, even? Crew? No. We worked pretty much autonomously and since my stuff was simple and straightforward, really only required me. Oh, and a babysitter, grumble, mumble. Just because the others had harder, bigger cases to solve and needed backup— not supervising, grouse, snarl—didn't mean they were keeping me in the dark on purpose.

Except I knew they were. Growl.

When Crew tried to join me at the lodge, I sent him to bed.

"You're no good to me yawning at everyone," I said. "Besides, if today is like yesterday, I've got things under control."

"What about the inspector from the PI Board?" Crew wasn't fighting me as I pulled his t-shirt off over his head and tugged the covers of the freshly made bed back while he slid free of his jeans.

"Dad sent Lance packing and I can stall long enough if he does show up to call you and have you meet me." Crew sank back on the pillow, Petunia heaving herself up the steps at the end of the bed to join him. "So, it's fine. You need to sleep." I bent, kissed his forehead, his lips, lingered a moment.

He didn't argue past the point of passing out in mid-inhale, Petunia happily taking my spot in bed, on my pillow, with her back pressed into his chest. The fact my fat pug liked to spoon my husband made me grin as much as it made me jealous.

Speaking of not sharing info, Dad was waiting for me in the lobby at the lodge when I arrived, something Crew clearly knew nothing about.

"Bet you're excited to work with your old man." Dad prodded me with his elbow before grinning, clapping his hands together and rubbing the palms with a rasping sound in anticipation of what, exactly? Did he know how boring today was going to be?

He did. And he loved every second of it. So maybe I wasn't cut out for this after all.

Oh, stop it, you drama queen.

Demo day started with another speech, though considerably shorter this time, Doris taking her turn at 9AM to begin the day.

While most of what she said pertained to technical details and conference rules, as well as a review of the schedule of teaching opportunities and information outlets, she finished with a rather emotional wrap-up.

"Every year I do my very best to ensure this conference not only happens but is a success. And every year, despite last-minute issues, struggling to find sponsors," wasn't lost on me Gavin was the center of attention when she said that, nor on him, since he grinned and waved at those who glanced his way, "and venues, this convention has never once failed to give you the opportunity to share your creations with the world."

"Right, because small venues like this one are the world." I turned to find Gavin had sidled up to me, winking and grinning in that charming way of his. "Poor Doris. So deluded."

I didn't find him funny, considering my commiseration with the older woman. He must have realized it because he backed off instantly, a faintly apologetic smile not helping.

Okay, so I was grumpy after all. Maybe it would sharpen my focus.

A smattering of applause met Doris's finish, though I missed her final words thanks to Gavin's interruption. Whatever she'd said hadn't had the desired effect—or did, depending on what her goal had been—and as everyone split and went their own ways, booths at the ready for day two. I wondered how such a mismatched and unhappy group of people could continue to gather this way since they all seemed to dislike each other so much.

Even Nicole and Teddy seemed to be on the outs this morning. I almost approached to say hello and assure Nicole I was watching out for her, but it didn't seem worth it when she parted from him with heated words, their distant conversation leaving him frowning after her before he stalked off and left the room.

I turned, writing off the option of talking to Nicole just then, and almost ran right into Callie who hovered at my shoulder silently. It was obvious she'd been watching her mom and Teddy argue from the sad look on her face and when she sighed, I knew she had her own hopes and dreams when it came to the pair.

"I just wish he'd tell her he loves her," she said in a tiny voice, offhand like she didn't know she was speaking out loud, "and that Mom wasn't still in love with Blake."

She drifted off toward her mother's display, leaving me with my skin crawling at the thought of anyone loving him—even that rigid wife of his—and sorrow for the girl who just seemed to want her mother to be happy.

CHAPTER FIFTEEN

I FOLLOWED AT A distance, keeping ten feet between me and Blake Hughes while he made his rounds, not out of respect or anything, just the sheer need to ensure his yuck didn't rub off on me in the sustained duration of our interaction.

He only got worse with time, not better.

Today's demo opportunity provided inventors with a chance to have him take a look at their pitch, their creations and their business plans up close and personal. I hadn't realized it, but part of the money they paid to register went to Blake and his song and dance pony show which, I quickly decided after watching him peruse the first of the twenty-odd inventions, amounted to about bupkis. Oh, right, and a slowly building headache for yours truly fed by my crushing need to shoot him down while doing everything in my power to keep my Fleming mouth shut.

It was a paycheck, nothing more, and his lack of authenticity and likely humanity had nothing to do with me.

At any other time, I would probably have failed to refrain from commenting, but I knew how much rode on this job and that all it would take would be a misstep on my behalf to bring my budding career to a crashing and fiery end. So, I traded my smart mouth and opinions on the matter of taste and propriety in favor of living to investigate another day.

So. Freaking. Hard. And more frustrating by the moment. If he wasn't such a caricature of a person, it might have been easier. Instead, the further he got into his glory, the more painful the experience of ghosting him became. I considered leaving him to his own devices and skirting the periphery of the crowd instead, but I knew I needed to stay visible if only to uphold my end of the bargain with Doris Campster.

Torture never felt so excruciating as observing his interactions with the creators he encountered. In fact, if he wasn't insulting them ("How could you possibly market such an unprofessional design?", or their pitches, ("No one will listen to that kind of drivel for even the thirty seconds you have."), or their business plans, ("Your projections are so terrible I can't imagine anyone would be willing to fund you."), he was pontificating on how he'd done things and how amazing he had been and how, if he had it to do over again, he'd nail it just like he did the first time.

The only time. Arrogance at its finest, ladies and gentlemen, step up and see real ego in action.

Maybe I could have brushed off his obvious pomposity if it wasn't for the simpering way his wife hovered and looked down her disdainfully pointed nose at everyone, offering an occasional snort of derision, like he was a visiting king gracing everyone with his presence and she his queen due their respect and admiration. Mind you, she did stay glued to her husband's side, so it was possible she understood she had no value without him. Either that, or she was well aware of Blake's wandering eyes (and hands and everything else) and was simply positioning herself to keep him in line.

A bit of both, perhaps.

Dad was nowhere in sight, though I knew he hadn't abandoned me. Surely, he'd let me know if he had to go? I did spot him a time or two, circling the room, but such sightings were few and far between so I could only assume he was here for me while doing other work, likely online, so he could satisfy as many clients as possible while making sure I had the backup I needed.

I could hardly blame him. This was his business, after all, whether my name was listed as co-owner or not. And I knew it meant a lot to Dad for me to take my place as his partner. His lingering guilt over not supporting my desire to go into law enforcement had to trouble him yet, though he'd done it with the best of intent. With any threat to my pursuing a job in the field long gone with the events of the past, he'd always expressed excitement at me joining him.

Still, it would have been nice for him to be present and accounted for if he was going to be here.

Doris, on the other hand, hovered between me and Blake, watching carefully and wincing slightly at every pronouncement of judgment on his part. Was she second-guessing her choice to make him keynote and to bring him in to adjudicate? It certainly looked that way. It couldn't be easy, her job, so I gave her the benefit of the doubt that she was being honest when she said she only ever did her best to ensure the convention happened and let her beat herself up. She didn't need my help in that category.

Elise Steel seemed bored with the proceedings, snarling occasionally at Gavin who also followed the wandering pack observing and taking in Blake's critical condemnations. The pair seemed to repel one another, though I could tell when Gavin grinned and purposely took a few steps closer to Elise, triggering her angry response, he enjoyed teasing her.

Not my problem or my business and, to be honest, kind of funny to watch and, trust me. The distraction was welcome.

We had just stopped in front of Nicole's display when Dad appeared at my elbow, towering over me like he always did, looking very professional in his dark suit. I'd only ever seen him dress this way when he went to weddings, so to have my normally casual father—or sheriff uniformed Dad—suddenly wearing such attire on a regular basis, white shirt and nice tie and shiny shoes and all—felt like I'd wandered into an alternate Universe where Dad wasn't really my dad but some kind of replacement who'd done things and seen things that my normally level and unshakable father could never imagine.

But when he smiled down at me, lighting his blue eyes, that familiar adoration I'd always felt from him in his gaze, I smiled back and resisted the urge to hug him, knowing it wouldn't look professional but wishing I could anyway.

Flaws and deceptions and secrets and all, I loved my dad.

"What have we here?" It was the first time Blake seemed happy to see one of the inventors and I had a feeling I knew why. Nicole blushed, smiled back, while Isobel's scowl of disgust and open dislike filled in the rest of the story. "Nicole Powell, how delightful. What do you have for us this year, my dear?"

His hand on her elbow, he guided her toward her own invention, though Nicole backed off as she described it to him, circling to the rear of the *Lighting In A Bottle* display, letting Blake take the front business end. I only vaguely paid attention to the spiel, since I'd heard it from her before, gaze scanning the crowd and the mingling inventors, some of whom scowled their obvious jealousy at the treatment Nicole received.

Playing favorites, Blake? How transparent of you.

"Now," he said in his booming voice, turning toward the rest of us with his hand outstretched, "let's see how a real inventor does things." With that, he flipped the switch.

Lightning showed up, all right, but not in the bottle. Nope. It found a new, unhappy home in the twitching, suddenly smoking and wide-eyed form of Blake Hughes who groaned a soft and oddly apologetic sound before his entire body went rigid and he fell to the carpet in a thudding collapse that spoke of dead weight.

No pun intended.

As the screaming commenced—not mine, for once—was it wrong I was actually happy not to be the only one to find the dead guy this time?

CHAPTER SIXTEEN

JILL WAS HER TYPICAL calm and collected self as she took my statement, already finished with the weeping Isobel, stunned and shaken Nicole and Teddy Kring who hovered behind the woman he loved and looked like he was going to be sick any second now.

"Thanks, Fee," the sheriff said when I told her everything I knew, including about Nicole's concerns someone was in the ballroom early this morning, that Ross Mullen had the list of those who'd entered and that if this wasn't an accident—Dr. Aberstock's determination yet to be delivered—it was possible someone sabotaged Nicole's invention for just this reason.

"Speculation," I shrugged. "But you know me."

She laughed, soft enough to keep it between us, because *decorum*. "I do," she said, eyes sparkling. "We'll see what the doc says. I'm going to talk to your dad." She left me then and I crossed to where Dr. Aberstock was stepping back from the body, now draped in a white sheet, two paramedics loading what remained of Blake Hughes onto a gurney for transport to the morgue.

"Fee!" The doc gave me one of his Santa Claus smiles, round cheeks pink, blue eyes twinkling, white beard and mustache perfectly trimmed into his short, shining hair. I always liked the doctor, had come to adore him over the last few years as he had been one of the few people in Reading who never once questioned or doubted me, Crew, Dad. He patted my shoulder, sighing, watching the EMTs wheel Blake away. "We always seem to see each other over dead people."

I choked on that. "Tell Bernice we'd love to have you for dinner," I said. His sweet wife was as much Mrs. North Pole as he was the ho-ho-ho man himself.

"We'd love that, Fee," Dr. Aberstock said. "Now, you want to know if this was murder or if the poor man was simply unfortunate, yes?" I nodded. "I can tell you, it wasn't an accident." He pointed to the invention, and it was clear even to me the switch itself had been the conductor of electricity from its blackened and melted appearance. "Unless this creation was so horribly designed as to intentionally supply a heart-stopping shock, I'd say you're looking at a saboteur. But don't take my word for it, my dear. The forensics boys will be here shortly."

"Thanks, doc," I said, "but you've never steered me wrong in the past. You say it's murder, I go killer hunting."

He smiled at me, worry in his eyes. "Please just make sure you take care," he said. "I do get rather miffed with you when you put yourself in danger and require my services for the living."

"Better than your slab and an autopsy," I said, trying for funny and landing so far off the mark I might as well have lobbed it toward the next town.

Dr. Aberstock shook his head at me. "So much like your father. I'll be at the hospital doing the postmortem if you have questions." He left with a wave for Dad and Jill and I realized he did so trusting I'd share what he told me with them while I choked up a little.

Because that vital word meant everything to me. Dr. Aberstock trusted me.

Okay then.

Olivia hustled toward her sheriff, and I joined her just as she corralled Dad and Jill off to one side, her olive-skinned complexion sallow with stress.

"I've made it official, pushed it through the council." She hooked her hand through my elbow and tugged me in tight, our huddle unbreakable with Olivia in control. "Fleming Investigations have permanent deputization status, all employees perpetually invited to contribute to any major crimes occurring in Reading upon request of our sitting sheriff and mayor." She shot Jill a glare. "I'm asking. Are you?"

Jill's shock was so obvious it took her a moment to respond. When she did, it was with a frown she fought to hide. I winced internally, knowing that yet again Olivia succeeded in making her own sheriff feel inadequate, though Jill's attitude shifted almost immediately when she spoke at last. "Of course," she said. "Help is always welcome.

Was it, though? When she pulled free of Olivia and backed off, I had to wonder how happy she was to have help. Not that Jill didn't love us, but she was sheriff. Man, this town.

I really didn't envy her that badge she wore.

Crew appeared, the only person, I figured, who could force Olivia to widen the circle just then, though perhaps if my mother showed up the mayor wouldn't have batted an eyelash. No matter, we quickly filled my husband in on what happened before I informed them all of what Dr. Aberstock told me.

"I'll have a look," Dad said, "but if Lloyd says it's murder, it's murder."

"I figured as much," Olivia grumbled. "What ever is wrong with our town?"

So I wasn't the only one who wondered? Good to know.

"Mayor Walker." Rose's voice penetrated but did nothing to part the waters. "Mayor Walker!" Strident little thing, wasn't she?

Olivia sighed and eye rolled before turning

toward the deputy. Surprise, surprise, Rose wasn't alone, Robert behind her, glaring at all of us like he knew exactly what was going on and hated us for it. "Yes, Deputy Norton?"

"If you're deputizing Fleming Investigations," she said, clearly with an ear to the ground at town hall if she heard what happened and got Robert here this fast, "then surely you'll choose to do the same for Carlisle Investigators."

Olivia laughed in her face. Now, I wasn't expecting her to say yes or anything, but the mayor was a political animal. I certainly wasn't anticipating the level of vitriolic animosity in Olivia's amused rejection, however. "You can tell Mr. Carlisle," she said, voice vibrating with anger, "he wasn't welcome in Reading when he was taken into custody and nothing—nothing, deputy—has changed in that regard."

Whoa.

"I could use a good investigator." Since when had Gavin Baker been eavesdropping? I guess I shouldn't have been surprised, though I was when he offered his hand to the startled Robert and shook my hateful cousin's with enthusiasm. "To protect my interests. Just in case someone is trying to kill me, too." He beamed a smile at me, then winked. What was he up to?

Robert seized the opportunity, and I knew he'd wring every last bit of life from it if it killed him. Chest puffed out not even close to reaching the girth of his potbelly, straining the buttons of his shirt against the round basketball he wore above his belt, Robert wriggled his disgusting mustache at all of us before nodding to his new client.

"I'll need all pertinent information, Sheriff Wagner," he said like he expected her to give him grief and just try to hide anything from him.

"Oh, you'll get it," she snarled. "All of it." Her gaze swept over her simpering deputy. "You're officially on permanent office duty, Norton. Now." With that, Jill stalked away from us and went to continue her interrogations while Rose flapped her lips in protest and then, pouting, flounced off.

And, to top off the delightful events of the morning, Lance Dustin chose that moment to appear, likely at Robert's prompting, his shock and dismay at the unfolding investigation making him seem rather innocent in my opinion. What, had he never been to a murder scene before? Dude had so much catching up to do.

At least he couldn't say I wasn't being supervised.

I avoided talking to him, only because there was a sudden outburst, Nicole's voice echoing. "That's impossible!"

Jill was asking her questions, so she must have brought up the switch. I joined them, choosing to do my job over giving either Lance or Robert a moment more of my attention, just as Nicole broke down into tears.

"I swear," she sobbed. "I didn't kill him. I would never." She turned toward me when she noticed I was there, reaching for me with shaking hands. "Ms.

Fleming knows. There was someone in here this morning. They must have sabotaged my invention. Killed Blake on purpose."

"How convenient," Gavin said. Laughed. Walked away.

While I watched him go, fully intending to find out just who Gavin Baker really was.

CHAPTER SEVENTEEN

WE HUDDLED IN THE back hallway of the lodge near the emergency exit leading to the ski lift. I'd had a rather unpleasant encounter with this part of the resort before, though it felt a lifetime ago and was a far different time of year. Still, I couldn't help the goosebumps that traced up my arms while Dad glanced up to make sure we hadn't been followed.

"Should we be worried about this Lance guy, John?" Crew's level tone of voice did nothing to hide the pulse of his heartbeat jumping on his neck nor the faint rise of another vein in the center of his forehead, sure sign my husband's temper was on the incline.

"I spoke to my contact," Dad said, deep voice

low and quiet, contained only to us, "on the PI board. Turns out Lance is a new hire, looking to make a name for himself after a string of failures of his own. Robert must have gotten to him." My father shook his head, sighed. "Poor kid, I really did like him once. But not my problem he couldn't keep a deputy job. Kept screwing up, and not small stuff, either. From what I hear, his last termination came from a chain of evidence issue that ended in a murderer walking."

Yikes. "So, this is going to fire him up," I said.

Dad didn't comment on that specifically. "We need to play by the book." He didn't sound happy about that. "My contact was pretty clear that someone is looking for a reason to shut us down, and not just Fee." He had been right. Dad didn't seem worried, at least on the outside. "We'll sort it out. For now, though, it's all hands on deck until the convention is over and Lance makes his ruling Monday morning."

"Good thing Liz's case wrapped." Crew nodded. "Everything else can wait, right?"

Dad didn't answer right away, a faint frown creasing his forehead, but he finally just shrugged. "It'll have to," he said. "The big issue, from what I understand, is that Fee's two years of experience is being questioned."

"Despite her track record as an investigator," Crew said.

"An unproven track record." We'd missed him sneaking up on us. Lance didn't seem aggressive or anything, but he'd clearly come to cause trouble, hands in the pockets of his too-large overcoat, his face set and determined. Dad stepped aside to allow him to join us which he did after a brief moment of hesitation. "Ms. Fleming was never officially an investigator."

"The fact you're leveling unfair scrutiny on her that you didn't on the rest of us sounds like someone has it in for Fee," my husband said. "Your friend Robert isn't doing you any favors here, you know."

Lance's lips twisted into a grimace like he already knew that. "The fact remains both you and Sheriff— Mr. Fleming are trained law enforcement and have many years of experience under your belts. You were both granted full licenses without the sixty-day trial period out of respect for your decades with both federal and local police forces." That did make sense to me. "I'm not out to get anyone, John, no matter what you might think of me." Lance sounded genuinely unhappy about my father's judgment. "The truth remains that your daughter has had no formal training aside from bumbling her way through solving a handful of cases that she shouldn't have been involved in in the first place."

Hit too close to home. "You're forgetting I was a deputy," I said, "and sheriff of this very town, Mr. Dustin. And that handful of cases? Try sixteen." Yes, I was counting the dearly departed young woman I'd never had the chance to meet and her poor infant. "Like it or not, whether I was invited to investigate or not, I'm a co-owner of a successful private investigation firm and I have a history of getting the job done."

And he was so right on all of the counts he'd brought up I knew I didn't have a leg to stand on. Still, Lance seemed to consider what I'd said before nodding.

"It would seem I've been supplied with biased information." Lance's hesitation was at least partially gratifying. "I need to dig further into what happened before I can make my ruling."

"Whatever you decide," Dad said, "we have a job to do, and we've been hired by the town to assist in this investigation. Including Fee." He crossed his arms over that broad chest of his, looking down at Lance without animosity but clearly expecting to get his own way. "She is, as you can see, fully supervised and can use her prior experience to assist in finding the murderer. I don't see how that's something you could oppose."

Lance glanced at me, at Crew, back to Dad, clearly torn. "Fine," he said. "But I'll be observing Ms. Fleming's work as you conduct your investigation and if I am in any way concerned with how things are unfolding, I'll be asking the board to not only reject her license but review yours and Mr. Turner's as well."

Dad's face darkened, arms falling to his sides. "I'd be careful, Lance," he said in that deep and quiet voice that screamed run and hide, little boy. "Whoever it is sent you on this witch hunt, they won't win. And you just got this new job."

Lance flinched, took a step back, paling to ghostly white before he spun and walked off, though there was a distinct stagger to his first step that said weak in the knees.

"Nailed it, John," Crew said before turning back to both of us, now visibly upset. "Business as usual?"

Dad watched Lance go with the intensity of a gunslinger preparing to draw at noon before he nodded. "It'll be fine," he said. "Let's go solve a murder."

We returned to the lobby as a team, all three of us coming to a halt at the sight of Jill, one hand around Nicole's upper arm, as the sheriff led the inventor toward the main doors. I hurried to join them, Dad with me, Crew lingering on the outskirts of the conversation, and put myself between the two women and the exit.

"Tell me you don't think Nicole did this," I said, keeping my voice low so as not to cause Jill trouble, though I knew just standing here in her way looked bad. "Jill, no one is that stupid."

My friend's scowl in reply was all I needed. "I have more questions," she said. "If you'll excuse us." She bypassed me, Nicole turning her head to plead with me with big, terrified eyes while Teddy hurried in her wake. Whatever was up with Jill, I'd have to deal with it later.

At least she'd be busy questioning the one person I was pretty sure didn't murder Blake Hughes. I waited for Jill to leave before joining Dad who towered over Deputy Kit Somersby. She didn't seem intimidated, at least, so my father was playing nice.

Before I could join them, someone touched my arm and I stopped, Callie Powell openly weeping.

"Please help my mom," she said. "She didn't kill him."

"I know." I slipped my arm around her shoulders, leading her away from the crowd milling about in the middle of the foyer. I tucked the two of us in beside one of the six-foot white vases that housed towering glass plants, at least partial privacy provided. "Callie, I have to ask you some questions and I need the truth."

She nodded, wiping at her face with both hands, swiping at her nose with the cuff of her hoodie. "I won't talk to the cops," she said. "But if you ask, I'll tell you what you want to know."

See, it paid to be a PI. "Why were you in the ballroom last night? Sorry, early this morning?"

Callie's jaw jumped, eyes widening before she glanced sideways like someone might overhear before she sagged against me, lips a thin line.

"Anything but that," she said.

Oh boy. "Did you sabotage your mother's invention to hurt Blake Hughes?"

That got an instantaneous negative reaction, headshake and gasp of air while she clutched at me the answer I needed.

"I didn't kill him," she said. "I don't know who did. I just know Mom wouldn't't."

No matter how I asked, what I tried over the next few minutes, Callie refused to budge or tell me anything else about her reason for being in the ballroom. I finally let her go when Dad gestured for me to join him and Crew, watching Callie retreat to the elevators and likely her room upstairs.

"Anything useful?" Dad didn't seem hopeful.

"Not yet." I shrugged off my frustration. "I'll figure it out."

"I know you will." Dad turned to Crew. "Let's divvy up jobs for now, rather than follow each other around."

"Good idea." Crew smiled at me. "You, my love, are a crack at finding things online. Feel like giving research a go?"

Okay, so they'd already talked about this, had they? This whole conversation was an elaborate plan, a ruse, to lure me out of the field and into the office, to a desk and safety and out of Lance's way.

I let them have their deception, though I made sure they both bore the brunt of a level stare that told them I was onto them before I nodded.

"You two go question suspects," I said, like I was the boss. "I've got digging to do." And, with that, I gathered together the scraps of my dignity and left, refusing to show the disappointment I was feeling I'd been relegated to my desk.

CHAPTER EIGHTEEN

PETUNIA SETTLED NEXT TO me in the plush dog bed that had been Dad's gift to her on our first day at Fleming Investigations. I was aware he happily shared snacks with her that weren't good for her when my back was turned, his own addiction to Mom's chocolate chip cookies and other fine-baked items generously doled out to the dear old pug. I stopped commenting, partly because I knew Dad had a special place in his heart for her, seeing as she'd been his mother's dog, and partly because she'd been through so much, and I wanted to make sure no matter how much longer I had with her—be it short or forever—she had only happiness to look forward to.

That didn't mean I was going to let her health

suffer, though. I reached down to pat her, those big, brown eyes watching me with loving adoration, and decided I would talk to Dad. While cutting her off entirely didn't seem fair, letting her become unhealthy wasn't an option either.

Right, because the next time she moon-eyed at me for a bite of something I'd say no. She owned me and everyone else she came across, the brat.

Petunia devoured her treat of fresh blueberries while I opened my laptop and dug into the interesting and rather convoluted world of inventions and patents. My list of names generated its own plethora of fascinating information, namely three things that raised my eyebrows and had me *hmmming* to myself.

First, and the quickest to pop up, was the fact Teddy Kring had an assault charge against him and had served three months (over weekends) in jail followed by four thousand hours of community service for assaulting another man. Mind you, it was years ago, and yet his propensity for violence wasn't lost on me.

The fact he was also an electrical engineer and in love with Nicole who pined for Blake for some (as yet to be explained to me so I'd understood it) reason, and I had a viable suspect for the murder.

However, the sticking point remained that killing Blake using Nicole's invention meant she'd be in hot water, as had come to happen. Would Teddy have put the woman he cared about in such a position or found a more physical and personal means of doing away with Blake if that was his intent?

It was possible Teddy's affection for Nicole was a smokescreen and that he had some other grudge against Blake I had yet to uncover. But, for now, while he was on my list, he remained low and on simmer.

My second discovery was much more enticing. A rather impressive insurance policy had just been written against the death of Blake Hughes and, as these things tended to go, the sole beneficiary? None other than his dear, jealous and rather distasteful wife, Isobel. I'd come across murderers who'd killed for less than the ten million dollars she would receive. It was clear from her financials as well Blake's lingering success as an inventor had seen its day, their expensive house on the brink of foreclosure and several final notices on large ticket items red flags in my opinion.

She'd been in the room, had access, motive. Surely, she knew her unfaithful husband was making a fool of her behind her back. Another excellent motive for murder. Electrocuting someone was a rather feminine way to kill, too, at least from my past research. Men tended toward the abrupt and physical when it came to ending another person's life. Women liked to keep their hands clean in more subtle forms of corpse creation.

The problem was, she had no formal training in electronics and, from what I could tell of her past, had zero history of interest or engagement with the invention community. Sure, she could have learned what she needed to know to kill Blake from observation, but it was more likely if she was the culprit, she'd hired out.

That meant there was a possible assassin for hire still unidentified.

Okay, so I loved this part, the mental gymnastics of digging and jigsaw puzzle building and tearing down ideas I'd just built in favor of others. Maybe Dad and Crew had been right to send me to the office to fill this role.

Not letting them off the hook completely or anything, but yeah.

Maybe.

The third tidbit of information I uncovered shortly thereafter made me stop and consider the next alternative. Gavin Baker had several outstanding lawsuits against him, but from what I could tell they were all civil cases, not one criminal or private case ever holding up in court. It was clear from the number of filed and failed cases that Gavin wasn't a straight shooter. Could Blake somehow have uncovered something to change all that, triggering Gavin to kill him and keep him quiet?

I was reaching, yes. Nothing indicated any connection of that sort, and yet. I'd learned to never discard an idea, just in case something came of it down the road. Most of the cases I'd been part of—and solved, truth be told—had resolved in the least likely manners because of deceits I'd overlooked until the last moment.

To my surprise, when I checked into Doris

Campster, I discovered she had been an inventor herself. I don't know why that shocked me, except she seemed more the organizer type than the creative. Still, it did make sense that she used to dabble in inventions, considering her passion for the convention she ran. Interesting, and made me wonder why she gave up so abruptly what looked like twenty years ago after a newspaper article announced she'd be selling her revolutionary water turbine design to a major corporation.

I'd never seen the like of it before, and when I tried to find out what happened, why it never came to fruition, I met a dead end and more than a little frustration.

If she sold the invention, what happened to it?

The door to the office opened, entry chiming, welcoming Dad and Crew. Toby had the weekends off, and there was no way I was running coffee for the two of them. I'd made that pretty clear from day one, which meant they instead carried three large cups from Sammy's, my darling husband depositing one in front of me with a smile and a wink.

Almost completely forgiven.

I filled them in on everything I'd uncovered so far, mentioning my suppositions as I always did, loving that neither of them argued with me, simply sat and nodded or frowned at the floor or sipped their java as they digested what I said. From Nicole calling me early this morning to investigating the list of people who'd entered the room to the disappointing footage from the security cameras, I finished with what I'd just found out about Doris before sitting back and letting the two brilliant men before me hash out the details.

"I had another peek at the footage," Crew said, shaking his head. "I have a buddy at Quantico that might be able to do something with it, but I doubt it'll help. Whatever the glitch in the system, the images are just too degraded."

"Disappointing," Dad said, "but we've done more with less in the past." He shared his own findings, delivered via Dr. Aberstock and an early report from forensics. "Turns out the invention itself wasn't the culprit," Dad said. "It was an overload that took advantage of a flaw in the design. Someone rigged the plug to deliver a surge of extra power when the switch was flipped."

That was interesting. "Nicole was frantic to check on her power situation early this morning," I said. "Though, if it was her, why mess with it when I was present?" Another reason to believe she was innocent. Twice stupid? Or maybe twice brilliant.

Nope, wasn't buying it.

"It was on remote," Dad said, "so whoever set it up not only had a good idea of how her invention worked but their own talents when it comes to wiring."

"In other words," Crew said, "all of the inventors and probably half of the people they brought with them."

Yeah, super helpful. Still, at least we had confirmation of cause of death and murder.

Dad's phone rang, my father grunting faintly and pulling it out of his jacket, thumbing the screen before raising it to his ear. "Liz."

Crew perked immediately, tense while Dad listened. The way my father's expression tightened, his blue eyes narrowing to slits, big body sitting forward while his gaze flickered sideways to my husband meant things with our FBI friend weren't going as well as they'd expected.

"Got it," Dad said. "Crew's on his way." Dad hung up. "She needs you in… the city." What, not even going to tell me where exactly? "The case just broke open, Marshall's in hiding." Who was Marshall? "Damn it, she wants both of us as backup."

"Then you have to go," I said. "And Jill and her deputies will have to solve the murder on their own."

"Fee." Crew leaned toward me, took my free hand in his. "We can't just abandon her like this." That was aimed at Dad, my husband's loyalties clearly torn.

"I know," Dad said. "But what else can we do?"

"Nothing," I said. "Crew made it very clear, despite the fact neither of you has told me anything about the case Liz is working on," way to get a dig in, Fee, "that this is a huge thing for us, for our company. And while I'd love to know the details," jab, slice, poke, "that can wait until you get back. After you fix what's wrong." No, I didn't like it, wanted all the details right now, thanks, and wasn't going to get them.

I could wait. This was partially on me, after all. I'd been complacent, let them carry on without pushing for answers. But no more secrets from now on.

"I'll tell Jill," Dad said, standing abruptly.

"No," I said, joining him, pulling Crew up next to me, "I'll handle Jill. You two go to help Liz. And I want a full report when you get there."

Dad nodded, sighed. "I'm sorry, kid," he said. "I didn't mean to cut you out. Neither of us did." Crew nodded. "But it's sensitive stuff, political." He met my husband's eyes. "We signed a non-disclosure with Liz."

So, it was connected to the FBI.

"That's all you had to tell me," I said. "I'm your partner. I understand. Git."

I watched the two of them go, heads together, speaking in hasty whispers, returning to my desk to gather my thoughts while the door chimed and sent the two men I loved most in the world into possible danger I wasn't privy to.

Yeah, happy thoughts were few and far between when I gathered up my pug and headed for the sheriff's office.

CHAPTER NINETEEN

I WAS ON THE way to see Jill, I swear. Then somehow I swerved instead of going straight and ended up in the one place I probably shouldn't have landed myself in my present state of mind.

Then again, as I perched next to Mom, sampling a cupcake she graciously shared with me while Petunia begged and moaned and shimmied for her own donation, it was, as always, gratifying to be on the receiving end of my mother's constant and never-wavering support and understanding.

"Sweetheart, this is utter nonsense." She finished icing the large tray of vanilla cakes, dabbing a tiny sugar rose in the center of each, handing me a shaker of edible red crystals to use on the sweets while she finished off each with a pair of tiny green leaves. I did my best not to make a giant mess, though I didn't have my mother's finesse. "You're the only person, aside from your husband and father, even remotely qualified to investigate a murder." Mom looked up from her leaf application, sighing softly. "I never thought I'd ever say that," she said. "I only ever wanted you to be who you were meant to be."

"Thanks, Mom," I said. "I'm sure once Dad and Crew get Liz's problem sorted out, we'll be back on the job and this mess will all be behind us." I couldn't help the pout that pulled my bottom lip out of place. "It just sucks."

I didn't do sitting on my hands very well, in case you missed it.

"You're doing the right thing," Mom said, stepping back from the cupcake tray, blowing at a wisp of hair that had fallen free and across her cheek, hands sprinkled with icing and green food coloring. "Just steer clear of the investigation until your father gets back. The last thing you need is for Lance to make trouble for you." Right, she would have known him back in the day, too. So much I wasn't in the know about, so much I'd missed leaving Reading. Not blaming Dad for driving me away, but.

Dad. Blaming.

Mom frowned then, lips pursed.

"And Dad," I said. "Mom, do you know what the trouble is? Who might be making problems for him?"

She met my gaze with her matching green one closed off and flat, emotionless. Mom's years as a high school teacher and then principal had granted her the enviable talent to say volumes without saying a single word. From the way she held herself stiff but strong, stolid emotional state granting me nothing, she told me everything.

She knew exactly what was going on and why and I could just mind my own business for the time being.

The kitchen door swung inward, a slow-motion movement that revealed a visitor who clearly thought he might not be welcome. Well, he really wasn't, but Mom turned and smiled at Lance Dustin while I grunted in faint surprise to find out he was a guest here—of all places—and shimmied backward away from the cupcakes I'd just decorated, nodding to him as politely as I could.

"Mrs. Fleming," he said. "Ms. Fleming." Lance paused there a bit longer than was necessary and definitely in the uncomfortably awkward range until Mom tsked at him.

"Lance, dear," she said, "just come in already."

Really, Mom?

He joined us, slowly but with a rather determined look on his face. He'd shed the ridiculous overcoat that made him look so boyish and now stood, white shirtsleeves rolled up, tie loosened, dark dress pants at least fitted enough he didn't appear to be wearing something he'd grow into eventually. The animosity he'd originally carried for me seemed to have vanished, and even the intense need he'd shown to prove me incapable faded to concern, anxiety, but not aimed in my direction.

"I hoped to talk to John," he said. Glanced at Mom, then at me again. "He's not here?"

"He had to leave town," I said, "with Crew. Another case. So, I'm off this one for the time being." There, take that. Except I no longer felt like I wanted to push back against this young man. If anything, he seemed regretful, apologetic as he tucked his slim hands into his pockets, having trouble meeting my eyes.

"I see." Lance started as Petunia huffed over to him and sat on his foot, looking up with her usual eager anticipation for a treat. "Nice dog," he said.

I eye rolled and laughed, deciding to let him off the hook if he was willing to listen. "As long as you feed her."

He seemed startled by my response as if not expecting me to be kind. "Your father was right," he said, blurted, actually. Hey, that was my usual state of affairs. He stole my bit. "I was instructed your company has been operating outside of the law and that I was to find any means necessary to ensure your license didn't go through." He swallowed, Adam's apple bobbing. "And if I could come up with a reason to have John's revoked, I was to do so."

"By whom?" I leaned in again, Mom quiet but watchful, though she didn't try to intervene. So maybe she had information but didn't know herself who the threat was?

Didn't matter, ultimately, because Lance just shrugged, spreading his hands wide. "I don't know specifically," he said. "I received instructions by email from the board in general. I thought it was coming from everyone. But when we spoke earlier, when I made the connection to Robert, I decided to check into it." He sighed slowly and deeply, narrow chest hollowing inward as though he'd collapsed in on himself. "I'm sorry, Ms. Fleming. I really like your dad. He was a good boss. It wasn't his fault I got fired. He gave me every opportunity. I made the mistake of listening to Robert Carlisle years ago and I guess I'm still making it."

His anger was finally showing. Good for him. Spine and backbone and forthrightness and all that. Chin up, buttercup.

I should talk.

"If you find out anything else, I'd appreciate the heads up," I said.

Lance nodded immediately. "I've been looking through the cases you solved," he said, sounding equally impressed and jealous of my work. "Even without a license, you're a better investigator than a lot of people I've worked with." Was that a jab at Robert, perhaps? I chose to take it that way. "If you decide to ask Sheriff Wagner to be your supervisor for the rest of the case, or until your father returns, I won't get in your way."

"Thank you." I offered my hand without thinking about it and shook Lance's when he responded in kind. This time our handshake was firm and solid, respectful.

"I'd better be going," he said. "Please, tell your

dad I'm sorry. And I'll do some digging to see if I can find out what's really going on."

Mom handed him a cupcake. Lance grinned at her and though I knew he had to be close to me in age, he looked about fifteen when he did.

He left, munching her delicious baking while I watched him go with a soft thrill of satisfaction stirring my insides.

"Oh, Fee," Mom laughed, waving me off, "just go already."

She didn't have to tell me twice.

CHAPTER TWENTY

L ANCE'S SEAL OF APPROVAL acquired or not, I decided I still needed to play things safe just in case whoever was behind this little attempt to shut me—and maybe Dad—down decided to send another beast to do his or her bidding. That sent me to the sheriff's station where the new receptionist, Faith Harris, informed me Jill was gone back to the lodge, Nicole freed after being questioned for some time.

I thanked her and left, wondering if Jill finally found her replacement for Toby. When Dad started up Fleming Investigations, his faithful receptionist had fled to work for him, leaving first Crew, then Jill, to cycle through a long list of truly horrible candidates. But Faith seemed at least to have her head on her shoulders, smart enough to answer the phone correctly (don't even get me started on some of the people who tried to fill the job), clever enough to send me after Jill instead of to Rose who tried to overhear what I was saying from her desk in the bullpen, and nice enough to smile in seemingly genuine kindness, hazel eyes lit with it, light blonde ponytail professional enough over her sheriff's department issue jacket collar.

I headed for the lodge, not sure what to expect. After all, Jill had been acting a bit weird, ever since the interrogations started and Olivia made Fleming Investigations deputies with full access to the case—

Oh, Fee. Seriously? Was I really that stunned I didn't know exactly how this looked and what it meant to Jill and that, in doing so, the mayor had succinctly and callously undercut the authority of her own faithful sheriff? Of course, that was exactly the problem. I'd already considered the fact in the moment. While I knew Jill was a friend, it wasn't a huge leap to think she wasn't blaming Olivia at the moment but feeling a bit of a blanket hell no when it came to me, Dad, Crew. Her two former bosses—make that three if my brief stint as sheriff to her deputy counted—lording over her thanks to the mayor's agenda had to hurt.

No wonder Jill was short with me. I'd be pissed too if Olivia walked into my business and started making permanent changes I couldn't do anything about and had no say in altering.

The very first thing I was going to do on arrival?

Inform Jill Wagner, sheriff of Reading, Vermont, she was the boss, I was her lackey and whatever she needed? Just ask.

For Jill? I would fetch coffee and smile doing it.

The lodge foyer was bustling with visitors, but no one I recognized so I bypassed the check-in madness and headed for the ballroom. Kit stood at the doorway, looking like she'd been facing off with the whole world, harried and a bit frazzled but clearly with her sense of humor intact because she was able to smile at me when I joined her.

"Never a dull day, Fee," she said, though there were lots, thanks, and maybe I really was to blame for wishing for something exciting to happen. "You looking for the sheriff?"

I nodded, glanced at the doors behind her, but Kit shook her head.

"She was heading toward the elevators, last time I saw her." The young deputy stiffened when one of the inventors swerved in her direction, the woman's face tight with anger. "If you'll excuse me, I have another crazy person to tell they can't go near their stuff until the forensics guys are done."

I left her to the budding argument, narrowly avoiding being sucked in myself, dodging past a cluster of young people with small backpacks and trendy sneakers who looked ready to head out for a day of hiking.

If Jill had been elevator bound it would be hard to find her without just calling and asking where she was. I nipped into the bar for a moment to dial her number, noticing, as I did, Nicole's daughter standing near the counter, next to Elise Steel who sipped what looked like a martini with a sallow smile on her face.

Not that I was going to give the underage girl the boot for being here, but it seemed odd to me these two would be chatting. Though, as I scrolled through my contacts for Jill's cell, I told myself maybe Callie was trying to hire Elise to represent her mother. Then again, from what Faith told me, Nicole had left of her own power and without Jill appearing ready to lay charges, so there was no need for a lawyer at this point, right?

And, since lawyers tended to specialize, would one who knew patents be the best choice in a criminal proceeding?

Curiosity at full mast now, I slipped my phone back in my pocket and closed the distance between us because nosy never failed me in the past.

"You won't be disappointed," Callie was saying as I sidled up to the pair as quietly as possible, smiling when Elise noticed me immediately, the teenager turning in surprise and then dismay, to find me standing there.

"I was hoping to talk to you further, Callie," I said. "Please, don't let me interrupt, though. I can wait."

"We're done." She stuttered through those two words like I'd caught her with her hand in a cookie jar that wasn't hers before she nodded to Elise and hurried off, head down and hands jammed in her pockets so deep her shoulders rounded forward.

I waited for Callie to exit fully before returning my attention to the lawyer, offering her a steady and empty smile but nothing else. I'd discovered that being quiet often led others to speak out of turn. In this case, however, Elise simply downed the last of her drink before standing, tossing a couple of bills on the bar.

"I've already spoken with Sheriff Wagner," she said, drawling that out as if she'd been exonerated and I was wasting my time. Wasting hers, way worse. "If you'll excuse me." And, with that, she strolled out past me, more stork on stilts than woman and yes, I was annoyed, and thinking about her that way made me feel better.

No judging.

Meanwhile, I had a horrible feeling growing inside me that had nothing to do with murder and everything to do with the possibility Callie might be betraying her own mother to a third party. I barely knew the girl, but the creeping around in the ballroom after hours with no explanation, the animosity toward Nicole, the private conversation with a patent lawyer? Could Nicole be right? Could someone be trying to steal her work? And could that someone be her own daughter?

Only one way to find out. I headed for the foyer and the number for Nicole's room, determined to get to the bottom of this, at least, if nothing else. Only to run into Teddy Kring who, it appeared, had just argued with the rapidly retreating Callie.

"Looks like you had as much luck talking to her

as I did." I dove deep for empathy and succeeded, the tall engineer sighing as he watched the girl leave.

"She's her mother's daughter," he said. "Brilliant, stubborn and unwilling to accept anyone's help." Yeah, he didn't sound bitter or anything.

"I'm sorry to hear that," I said.

Teddy shrugged, managed a faint smile. "You have questions for me, Ms. Fleming? I understand you are part of the investigation team?"

Okay, so my whole plan to fall at Jill's feet and beg her not to be mad at me while following the rules and not putting my livelihood or my dad in jeopardy went out the freaking window like always as I nodded in response.

Hey, he offered.

"I'm sorry to bring this up," I said, "but I understand you have a record. Assault, wasn't it?"

Teddy shifted his weight from one foot to the other, embarrassment crossing his face. "I figured someone would dig up that old news," he said, keeping his voice down. "It was a long time ago. I was twenty-two, the guy was a friend who stole from me. Things got out of hand, and I paid for it."

"You're in firmer control of your temper these days, then?" I had to tilt my head back to look up at him, always hated the height advantage of tall men when I needed to be the one in the driver's seat. But he didn't try to bully me or argue, simply spreading his hands wide as if offering himself up for my careful scrutiny.

"Most days," he said. "Not always. I hate the way

Nicole kowtows to Blake, for example." He paused, swallowed, looked uncomfortable. "Kowtowed. I guess that's over now."

"Indeed," I said. "You're an electrical engineer, right?" He nodded instantly, absently, clearly lost in pondering the death of his rival. "Did you assist Nicole in the wiring or construction of the Lightning project?"

He rubbed one hand over his face, the harsh sound of palm on day-old stubble loud between us. "I helped in a few of the detailed components, but Nicole is a talented fabricator, so she did the bulk of everything herself."

"But you fully understand the workings of the invention, is that accurate?" Was he really that dense he didn't see where I was heading with this?

Apparently not.

"Ms. Fleming," he said then, voice flattening out and expression shifting to angry denial, "if you're implying I would, in any way, put Nicole or Callie in danger by tampering with her invention, you're crazy." He inhaled deeply, shoulders going back, posture set. "If I wanted to kill Blake Hughes, I would have found a way that didn't run the risk of harming people I care about." He blushed then while I reached out and patted his arm.

"I'm aware of your feelings for Nicole," I said.

Teddy spluttered, looked away, clearly unhappy with the turn of conversation. "Any more questions, Ms. Fleming?"

"Were you aware of any flaw in the design that

could have turned her invention dangerous under the right circumstances?" I was being vague, I know, but I didn't want to just hand him the information he might need to help Nicole escape justice if she was involved.

"I'd mentioned to her there was instability in the switch," he said, "but it's never been an issue."

She knew there was a possible problem. "Did anyone else know there might be an issue?"

Teddy shook his head, frowning. "It was a minor problem, easily fixed in the next fabrication. But Nicole ran out of time and, with extra insulation added, we assumed everything would be okay." He blanched then. "Was it an accident? Was this our fault for rushing to project?"

I hesitated before shaking my head, not wanting him to have to carry that around with him, or take it to Nicole, either. "We believe it was sabotage," I said, "but had to be someone who understood the invention."

Teddy nodded then. "Anyone with a grasp of electronics could have recognized the flaw," he said. "That means most of the people here, Ms. Fleming."

Just as I'd said to Dad not so long ago. "Thanks, Mr. Kring," I said. "You've been very helpful."

Yes, I could have pushed him further, but, like Nicole, I was pretty sure he had nothing to do with Blake's death. I wasn't done though, not yet. "Actually, I wanted to ask you if there's a reason why Callie would be speaking with Elise Steel." I paused. "About business."

Teddy's entire bearing changed, concern arching his tall body toward me, eyes tight and lips in a line as he closed the distance between us. "No," he said, "not as far as I'm aware. But Cal has been keeping secrets from her mother lately, in the last few months. Nicole's worried about her, and so am I."

"Worried about who?" Speaking of the devil's mother, Nicole joined us, clearly lost and a little dazed but with enough concern I knew she figured we were talking about her daughter. "Callie? What did she do now?"

I mentioned her talk with Elise while Nicole's worry only grew.

"I'll talk to her," she said. I held off mentioning the possibility Callie might have been negotiating to sell her mother's invention. Surely that thought crossed Nicole's mind or, if it hadn't, she had been through enough today she didn't need such things weighing her down further.

The truth would out soon enough. I just hoped it didn't mean a splintering of this family that wasn't.

"Nicole," I said, "I know you talked to Jill, but I have to ask, and I do so knowing you didn't murder him." She paled, nodded. "Did you kill Blake?"

She shook her head, clutching her arms tight to herself, hugging her own torso while Teddy hovered, his concern for her palpable. "I didn't," she said. "And I'll tell you what I told the sheriff, Ms. Fleming. I had no reason to kill Blake." She swallowed, looked up at Teddy, returned her attention to me. "Not considering Callie's paternity." Another short pause while I inhaled in surprise. "Blake was her father."

Whoa. What? The tall engineer at Nicole's side didn't flinch, so this wasn't a secret she'd kept from him. "Does Callie know who her father is?"

Nicole shook her head, a tight and rapid movement that freed most of her thin, dark hair from the fading ponytail she'd worn it in. "Blake would never acknowledge her and I didn't want her to suffer for that." Teddy appeared to disagree but kept his mouth shut as Nicole went on. "She thinks her dad died in an accident when she was a baby."

"You claim she's been secretive lately," I said, while both nodded. "Could it be she discovered the truth?"

Nicole's shaking exhale spoke volumes. "That's what I'm worried about." She met Teddy's eyes while he nodded to her to go on. "There was a blow-up at the last event, with Isobel. I confronted Blake and she found out about it. It's possible Callie overheard."

"Thank you," I said. "I'm going to have to talk to her eventually. Can you arrange that?"

Nicole nodded, clearly miserable. "I'll see what I can do," she said, turning and walking away, Teddy on her heels while I wondered what she'd ever seen in Blake when she had a kind and devoted man like that watching out for her.

Then again, my track record wasn't the best and we women? Seemed to like the bad boys for some reason.

CHAPTER TWENTY-ONE

WOULDN'T YOU KNOW, MY goal to find Jill was once again thwarted by my busybody tendencies to run into things that might or might not have been my business? Okay, not my business, no ifs, buts or ands. I knew better than to quibble over the truth at this point and it was a very rare moment that the things I stumbled on had anything to do with me.

Except, of course, I now had reason to be this nosy. My former status as busybody of Reading was no longer valid and though the faint nervousness of doing so lingered, the traces of memory that led me to wriggle at the thought of doing something outside my need to know, really had to take a hike.

At least, for as long as I was still an investigator,

or had the potential to be one. Poking my schnoz into the deep, dark secrets of others never felt so right.

My text to the sheriff went unanswered and, while I waited in the lobby for her to show, I couldn't help but notice Isobel and Gavin deep in conversation near the elevators. I had reason to stroll their way, right? Eavesdrop on their talk, find out if either of them had a further reason I had, as yet, to uncover to kill the deceased. The second Jill told me where she was, I'd be riding one of those to her side, so I needed to be at the ready.

Uh-huh. Good one, Fee. And unnecessary. I had a job to do, right?

Gavin cut off his chat with the widow, however, the instant I got close enough to overhear anything, grinning at me and shooting me with his thumb and index finger on the way by while he retreated toward the bar. I guess he was far too careful to get caught speaking out of turn. How else would he have been able to survive in this business as long as he had without constantly looking over his own shoulder? Heck of a way to live, but I wasn't judging his caution, just his choice of occupations.

Yup, judging that, you better believe it.

At least I knew where he'd be the next little bit because he and I had a conversation ahead of us. As for Isobel, I plastered on a smile, noting she was waiting for the elevator to take her wherever it was she was going, and I would lose her shortly.

"I didn't know you and Gavin Baker were

friends." Wrong direction to come from, I knew that instantly, but just couldn't stop the freight train of disaster chugging toward the widow from between my lips. "Interesting to discover you talking with one of your dead husband's least favorite people."

And exit stage Isobel.

Instead, she looked down that narrow nose of hers at me as the elevator doors chimed and slid open, disgorging a pair of hikers, leaving it empty and waiting for her. "Blake had a lot of enemies," she said.

"Apparently," I said, watching the doors close, elevator unused. "Was that why you took out that rather impressive life insurance policy on your own husband just three weeks ago?" She glowered at me, anger showing at last. "Ten million dollars is a lot of money, and ten million reasons for you to want your husband dead." I let that sink in a moment before going on while her color darkened further. "In case you missed it, Mrs. Hughes, a payout like that is an excellent motive for murdering a cheating spouse."

"Well, I never." She spluttered her fury at me while I waited for her to dig herself a hole. One I'd be happy to shovel dirt into once I had her down there, wallowing in her guilt while I wrapped up this case. Instead, she batted at the air between us as though she could make me go away with a gust of air from the waving of her hands, shooing me almost like a pesky fly. "That policy was Blake's idea. Here." She dug into her clutch with shaking hands, not a hint of remorse or anything resembling murderous intent showing, pulling out a business card and handing it to me. Well, if practically tossing it at me qualified. "I assumed someone would be asking about the policy. I know very well how bad it looks, Ms. Fleming." So much for *well I never*. "I retrieved that from my room and kept it with me." Her distaste for the conversation flared in a crumbling of her thin lips, edges bleeding red lipstick, skin sallow, dark circles under her eyes making her gaze appear sunken and rather demonic. "You can call Ms. Mansfield and ask her all about it. She's the insurance agent we used, the very one Blake himself hired for the job." I checked out the card for Sunbeam Insurance, name, phone number, email, cutesy byline and all, while Isobel went on. "My husband might not have been perfect, or entirely faithful, I admit as much. But I loved him, Ms. Fleming, despite his faults, and he loved me." I wasn't going to deny her that because I had my doubts, letting her instead finish without comment. "Think of me what you want, think of Blake as you believe you must, but I stood by him all these years for a reason that had nothing to do with money." Right. Because his fame and now misspent fortune wasn't the kind of lure she'd hang onto? Not buying it. "I had no reason to kill him."

"The insurance money will go a long way to paying off your debt," I said, refusing to back down when I had her in such a state. It might have been cruel, but I found people tended to spill more when they were upset, things they didn't mean to share.

"That's a very good reason."

Isobel didn't respond to that, going rigid. Since I was at this point with the suspect, I figured I'd just ride out the galloping horse on the way to the cliff's edge and dump everything I had on her.

"Not to mention," I said at my most deadpan while her face paled, "the child he refused to claim. That had to hurt." I paused for effect, noting her total lack of acceptance, the way she rejected with her entire being anything to do with Nicole's claim to Callie's birthright. "Oh, and wouldn't that mean there's a second heir to the policy?" Yes, indeedy doodle, it did. "My dear, how awful to have to share with his child from another woman when you've been so very faithful for so long for all the wrong reasons."

Wow, when did I become so vindictive and mean? Um, hmmm.

Kinda went with my temper, I guess.

The elevator doors chimed once again, and this time when they did, she entered after the small group of people who'd ridden it down departed. "I'm through speaking to you without a lawyer present," she said. "Good day, Ms. Fleming." She rather violently pressed a button on the bank before her, staring me down while the doors slid closed again.

Well now. She didn't seem all that devastated by her loss, did she? The insurance policy certainly was a rather damning bit of evidence at this point. Better believe I'd be calling Marsha Mansfield and asking her everything about the policy. Sure, it might clear

Isobel of suspicion, but I wasn't ready to let her off easy, not with this kind of proof in the offing.

Besides, I didn't like her. So suspect list it was, Izzy.

With no word yet from Jill—trust me, I checked my phone twice to be sure she really wasn't talking to me—I headed for the bar and Gavin Baker, ready to go to battle yet again, but of a different kind.

Yes. This was fun. I was going to hell in a handbasket for loving it so much.

CHAPTER TWENTY-TWO

TO MY SURPRISE, IT wasn't Gavin I encountered at the bar, but Doris Campster, perched on the same stool where Elise had sat, round body drooping over the edges and through the slats of the armrests, what looked like a neat scotch in a short glass before her.

She looked up when I touched her elbow, blinking at me. This clearly wasn't her first drink, though I hadn't seen her in here before.

"Minibar was empty," she said as if reading my mind. "How can my minibar be empty?"

Oh, dear. "Doris, I'm so sorry," I said, sitting next to her, hoping my compassion made it through the alcohol she'd consumed.

She patted my hand with a rather firm gesture,

sagging against the bar to sip her sorrows away. "Your sheriff shut down the rest of the conference," she said. "Olivia tried to stop her, but she insisted. And, I suppose, I understand. Agree with her, even. It's just..." she sighed into the glass, mist forming on the interior for a moment. "In ten years, I've encountered a lot of trouble." She giggled a little. "So many problems, grudges, people to wrangle. But I've never once had to shut down." She hiccupped softly, took another drink. "Not *once*." She set her glass down with a thunk, the slippery sides falling from her fingers at the last moment. "No one can leave town. Everyone's inventions are under lock and key. I can't get the deposit back." She sobbed once. "This is a disaster."

There wasn't much I could do to help, so I did what always worked and tried to distract her. "Doris, can I ask you a question about Gavin?"

She seemed to pull out of her funk, those eyes blinking slowly at me from behind her glasses again. "You want to know why," she said, voice low and hissing though everyone in the bar could hear her. "Why did I let him be a sponsor and take part. Is that it?"

Movement at the end of the bar caught my attention and I glanced up to find Gavin grinning at me. He saluted with his own glass but didn't try to interfere when Doris went on, oblivious to his presence or her own lack of decorum thanks to the scotch she'd drunk.

"She has an excellent reason to allow such a

person into the convention." I hadn't expected Robert to interrupt, to lean against the bar with his back to Gavin, dress jacket over his too-tight shirt reminding me just how pathetic and desperate Robert was for approval and that, by donning such attire, he made it utterly clear to me he still wanted Dad to respect him.

"Which is?" I was feeling particularly defensive and protective of Doris, not only because I knew she was in a crappy situation with no way out, but because my hated cousin dared to stand there with that smirk twisting the vile pornstache on his upper lip into a disgusting creature that I was sure would smother him in his sleep someday.

Today, please. Make it today.

"She's been aiding and abetting him in stealing patents," Robert said, "and burying the inventions."

She *what* now?

Doris twitched, flinched, gaped at him while my heart sank and I realized, for likely the first and only time in his miserable existence, Robert got something right.

"What is he talking about, Doris?" I gently turned her toward me, doing my best to stay calm and not let her see I'd suddenly lost all respect for her. It was clear if she wasn't part of Gavin's work, she knew about it because moisture rose in her eyes and she shook her head, pulling free of me, swallowing the last of her scotch in one big gulp.

"It's a thing, you know." Gavin finally decided it was time to join the party, though his smile hadn't faded, and he seemed irrepressibly confident. Which made me wonder if Robert was right after all. "Corporations sponsor patents—buy them as a contract from inventors who think it's a partnership but names the corp as the owner of the patent." He was far too amused by such activity for me to hold on to any semblance of good feeling toward him. "The corp pays the inventor a small retainer, claiming it's an advance, takes the patent and buries it to keep the invention from ever seeing the light of day."

"That's stupid," I said, knowing I let my anger show.

"Lucrative," Gavin said. "And perfectly legal. Not, however," he saluted Robert with his glass, sipping casually at the contents before going on, "what I do. No, my particular specialty is assisting inventors to do things for themselves. I'm merely a guide, a mentor. The people who engage creators that way? They're another level of miserable even I'm not capable of."

He sounded cocky enough to be telling the truth. "Why would a corporation buy a patent only to bury it?" It made no sense to me.

"Because they are buying up the competition," he said. "They don't care for innovation when they do it. They just want the competitor's creation to die so they don't have to change a thing or go to market against them. Simple economics."

Wow. "How common is this?" I ignored Robert who seemed frustrated his short attempts to break into the conversation were squashed as Gavin and I rapid-fire spoke back and forth, cutting out the annoying middleman.

"Common enough, though not so much now that message boards and groups have oversight available for new inventors." Gavin finished his drink, setting the empty on the bar, waving off the bartender who approached to give him a refill. "But it still happens to the young and unwary." He paused a moment as if going to say something else before shrugging like it didn't matter. "I might be accused of ripping off inventors, but I at least allow them to keep control of their product. Sure, my prices are elevated, but I have a living to make." He wasn't the least bit apologetic for that truth. "And the courts happily agree with me I've rendered services as promised, no matter what my former clients might claim."

I might not like it, but he had a point.

It was only then Doris seemed to fully fathom what Robert had accused her of because she chose then to spin on my cousin and toss the rest of her drink in his face. Robert cried out, fell back into Gavin, whose association with my cousin had clearly come to an end before this whole conversation began. Gavin pushed Robert off him, dusted himself clean of the contact, and bowed his head to me.

"How dare you accuse me of something like that." Doris muttered her way through the second half of her outrage, with enough alcohol in her system I was pretty sure she was going to have trouble staying upright let alone focusing in the next few minutes. "How *dare* you."

I'd misjudged her, repentant enough for my leap to believe Robert, I glared him down before slipping one arm around the older woman. "Let's get you to your room," I said. "You'll feel better after a bit of sleep."

"Would never," she whispered. "*Never.* Horrible thought. Hurtful thing. Never." She stumbled out of my grasp as she heaved herself off the stool, pushing me away when I tried to assist. I watched with vague horror as she meandered her way to the elevators and managed to board, doors closing behind her as the guilt I'd let her go alone kicked me in the butt.

Robert slipped away, skulking weasel that he was, while Gavin laughed. I confronted him, furious now, facing him down while he waved at the bartender for another drink. Changed his mind, had he?

"Why did you hire Robert?" I had more questions, obviously, but that one rankled the most.

"To stir the pot, dear Fiona Fleming," Gavin said before chuckling again, sitting in Doris's empty stool, patting the one next to him. "Buy a beautiful redhead a drink and tell her all about it?"

I really should have walked away. Sat down and huffed at him while he sipped what the bartender delivered, some mixed something that looked like soda and was likely not.

"You're not a nice man," I said.

He shook his head. "Not even a little," he said. Laughed again. Then sighed, tipping his drink toward me. "I know a loser when I see one, and your cousin there has waste of space written all over him. Figured

I'd add to the fun and see what came of it."

Seriously. Who was this guy? "So, you admit you con people, but you do it legally, is that it?"

Gavin sipped before answering. "I offer a service," he said. "If people don't do their homework and realize everything they pay me for they can do for themselves for free, that's not on me." His expression settled from amusement to resignation. "The law's on my side." He finished his drink quickly then, checking his watch. "Speaking of which, I have some calls to make. If you'll excuse me."

I let him go, knowing I had Blake questions to ask, but not wanting to be near him any longer. Sure, Robert was vile and revolting and I couldn't stand him. But someone like Gavin Baker?

I needed a shower just from sitting next to him.

That being said, when I checked my phone and realized Jill still hadn't deigned to get back to me—yes, I was getting angry now, because seriously, this wasn't my fault and she knew better—I huffed my way out of the bar in pursuit of the sheriff who would talk to me, damn it, if I had to hold her down and make her say uncle.

CHAPTER TWENTY-THREE

JILL'S AVOIDANCE GAME WAS better than my find-the-sheriff, apparently, because I finally gave up wandering the lodge in an attempt to track her down and instead headed back to the office for more research.

Because research was my best means of diffusing myself so I didn't go off on her when I saw her again. Don't waste my time.

Alone in the quiet of Fleming Investigations, I allowed myself to switch off my temper and, instead, turn on my inquisitiveness when it came to the wild and wacky world of inventions.

The process of patenting an idea seemed as simple as it was complicated and rather than make my brain bleed over understanding every nuance, I instead accepted the gist. It turned out the application itself wasn't so hard to do but having a working prototype and creating a marketing plan while waiting on a novelty search—or examination by the patent office if your idea was, in fact, unique and qualified for said patent—seemed part and parcel with the actual end result of gaining a patent. Doing so, however, was no guarantee of any success and, from what I understood from my reading, there were well over nine million U.S. based patents alone, with the bulk of those not only never making money, but the initial applications only making it to that stage and not to the final patent acquisition.

Fascinating and disheartening if one had their dreams set on being a successful inventor. And with time limits enforced between the initial sale of an invention and patent application meaning if you'd failed to file before a year was up, the inventor forfeited forever the right to apply.

It made me wonder why anyone would throw their hat into such a clearly failure-ridden profession. Then again, I was on my way to becoming one of over a hundred thousand registered private investigators. So, while my odds were better, they weren't that great, either, considering one good invention could make a career while I had a lifetime of digging into people's dirty secrets ahead of me.

Personally? I chose the latter.

As for the corporation buyouts, they seemed less popular than simply copycatting inventions, patented or not. Since most inventors weren't wealthy, large corporations and even reasonably sized businesses were able to rip off ideas and the inventors were left with the option to sue, but not the financial wherewithal to follow through.

The more I read, the more my anger returned. My disgust at the entire process finally drove me to slam my laptop lid shut and glower at the wall across from me like doing so could solve the problem.

Time to get some perspective. I opened my computer again and headed for the first message board I could find. Poking around in the common questions thread wasn't much help when it came to my temper, the majority of posts asking for help from the community on the very same topics. And again, while the burying of patents after purchase from corporations wasn't common, from what I could tell in old threads, it only seemed to have lost momentum once the internet's popularity allowed for inventors to talk to one another.

The downside? Rather than being sneaky about it, corps started openly stealing, their finance departments and legal divisions weighing the comparative costs of producing and selling stolen inventions versus the possibility of lawsuits.

While corrupt and despicable, that was business.

I finally opened a message in a chatroom and brought up Blake Hughes, just to see what would happen. I wasn't expecting the explosion of dislike and derision aimed at him. Everything from "disgusting pervert" to "total jerk" to "arrogant ass" seemed a revolving door of attitude I quickly shunted to one side in favor of focusing on those who might have information on why someone would want to kill him.

Wait, he's dead? That's horrible but couldn't have happened to a nicer guy. That from inventordad2910.

I heard he'd died, but murder? He's pissed off a lot of people, but murder? Mysterymeat334 wasn't helpful.

I couldn't stand the guy, but he wasn't worth going to prison for, roaminangelofinvention sent.

Since the rest of the responses I received mimicked them, I finally sighed and signed off, redheadofreading frustrated and needing a cookie.

I did, however, come across something I wasn't expecting, stumbling over the thread by accident and catching my breath at the content, especially when a name I knew very well popped up in the middle of it.

The lodge was a quick drive while I ordered my thoughts, room number easily acquired from the front desk. But it wasn't until I was standing in front of Nicole Powell, her surprise I'd knocked on her door showing for a moment, that I finally figured out what I wanted to ask.

"Did you know about the patent purchasing?" I held up a printed sheet with her name on it, nicolepowell70, complaining about the very thing.

Nicole gestured for me to come in, expression pained and eyes sad. "I can tell you anything you want to know," she said. "I'm afraid I know intimately just how devastating such an attack can be."

I entered the room, sitting on the edge of the bed

while she took the small office chair at the desk opposite, letting her have the sheet I'd printed when she reached for it.

"I was so innocent then," she said. "This thread is ancient, from almost twenty years ago." Nicole's faint smile was still regretful. "I was one of the founding members of the message board. For this very reason." She held up the page. "We've added to it over the years, along with a number of other things for new inventors to look out for. This one is about to be archived because it's not so common anymore."

"So, I've been told." The only reason I'd spotted it? It sat in prominence at the bottom of the screen, along with five others listing the major pitfalls.

"I fell for the glory line I was handed, accepted money, didn't find out until after the patent went through that the corporation that paid for it was listed as the owner. When I pursued them, they had their lawyer reply." She sighed softly, an old hurt. "When I talked to the patent office, they were empathetic but there was nothing they could do."

"From what I read Blake was involved." She'd mentioned his name, at least.

Nicole seemed startled by that, then shrugged, pushing a strand of hair behind one ear. "He'd made the introduction," she said. "The corporation rep took it from there. But it was my mistake and when Blake found out he was angry. But we were broken up by then. He was just trying to do me a favor."

So she said. Still, there was no animosity in her

toward him that I could sense, so I was again barking up a bush when I needed a tree.

"We broke up shortly before I found out I was pregnant." Nicole brushed at one cheek, and I realized she was crying, her voice thickening, head down over the page. "I blamed him for my mistakes for a long time, including Callie. I never wanted a child, at first, and when he refused to accept her as his, I cut ties with him for a decade. When I ran into him at a convention, he seemed to regret the distance, though he was already married to Isobel. I can't believe he had any ill intent toward me, despite the fact he refused to acknowledge his daughter."

That did seem to bother her, but not in a madly murderous way. No, instead her tears continued to trickle, guilt and old damage showing on her face, aging her past her late forties.

"The real problem isn't this," Nicole said, shaking the page at me, "but people like Gavin. And businesses that rip off ideas even after patents have been officially issued." I nodded, not bothering to tell her I'd uncovered the cycle of yuck that was her world.

"Could Blake have been involved in something that got him killed? A scam?" I knew better than to ask her, figured she'd brush off the question without giving it the benefit of the doubt.

Instead, Nicole paused, really seemed to think about it. "I don't know, Ms. Fleming," she said. "I honestly have no idea."

Part of me hesitated to talk to her about her

invention's role in the death of the man she still had feelings for, but I had to ask. "According to Teddy Kring, he warned you there might be an issue with the switch and safety?"

Nicole's whole body flinched. "I can't believe it," she said. "There's no way." She almost sounded like she didn't believe her own denial.

"Did anyone else know about the flaw?" I was giving her information, too, because she perked when I asked.

"You do think it was sabotage," she said.

No comment. Just answer the question.

Nicole's short-lived relief turned to doubt. "I don't think so," she said. "At least, not as far as I know." Her reticence to share details about her invention with me yesterday was a clear indicator of how she handled everyone around her, not to mention her paranoia. Since her invention had killed Blake thanks to tampering, she had every right to think the way she did, though. "They won't let me examine it," she said, a near wail in her voice. "I could tell them what happened if they'd just let me look at it. I'm sure it wasn't my fault."

She was right, at least as far as the forensics report stated, but I couldn't let her off the hook just yet.

I hadn't noticed the adjoining door to the next room was partially open and looked up as Callie entered. She appeared as distraught as her mother and rushed to hug Nicole. Startled herself, the inventor stood and embraced her daughter, the pair crying a moment as they hugged one another like I didn't exist.

It wasn't meant to last, though. Callie pulled away, face contorting. "He wasn't a saint, Mom," she said. She didn't seem to care her mother's invention was the cause of death, only that Nicole accept he wasn't the man she thought he was. "He wasn't a good person at all."

"Please stop saying things like that about Blake," Nicole shot back, visibly angry at the assault, likely due to the hope she and her daughter might have actually put things behind them.

Callie shook her head, still crying. "I won't," she said. "He didn't deserve you or your loyalty. You have no idea." She spun and ran out her mother's door into the hallway, Nicole swiping at her tears, about to go charging after her.

"Please," I said, hand on her arm, seeing her denial turn to shame and regret. "Let me."

Nicole nodded at last and sat once again as I headed for the exit and a long-overdue heart-to-heart with the teenager. She had secrets she was going to tell me and if she thought otherwise, she had another thing coming.

Man, did I sound like Lucy Fleming just then.

Callie hadn't made it far, barely to the door to the stairs, where she stood, shaking and staring at her phone. I cornered her, a fact she didn't realize until I had her pinned down just by the sheer proximity of my person, and though she looked like she wanted to push past me and run, she didn't.

In fact, she caved, I watched it happen, phone clenched tightly in one fist.

"Blake Hughes was a snake and a liar, and he stole from other inventors," Callie said. "And I can prove it."

CHAPTER TWENTY-FOUR

C ALLIE DIDN'T WAIT TO see if I was going to demand proof, whipping her phone up and showing me what she had. I took it from her, read through the pages and pages of accusations against someone named B.M. Howatt, accusing B.M. of copycatting, infringing and outright stealing ideas from small inventors. And yes, there was one complaint that claimed B.M. intentionally misled the creator into selling their idea to a corporation only to lose their patent.

"I take it you also have proof B.M. Howatt is Blake Hughes?" I gave Callie her phone back and, a few taps later, she held up a screenshot of a birth certificate next to a legal change of name document. Blakely Morton Howatt had petitioned the court in

1991 to change his name to Blake Hughes.

"I'm impressed," I said. "You should have my job. How did you find this?"

"Mom." Callie sniffled, shrugged, staring at the screen. "She thinks he was my dad. So I went digging."

Oh, crap. Callie *did* know. "I'm sorry your mother didn't tell you outright."

Callie shook her head then, sorrow gone into dull anger. "She might as well have told me my father was from outer space," she said. "Because Blake Hughes—or B.M. Howatt—wasn't my dad. I have no idea who is."

She seemed sure enough I nodded, making a leap at a guess. "You did a paternity test."

"DNA." She rubbed her arm with her free hand like she wished she could erase what she knew from her whole body. "I took a used tissue he tossed at the last convention and sent it away. Got the results last week. Confirmed what I already knew." She met my eyes, her own flatly empty. "Not my father. Thank god."

Well, I couldn't fault her for that attitude, considering. "Does anyone else know about Blake's other identity?"

Callie shook her head, thin ponytail wobbling, cheeks sinking inward as she sucked at her lower lip. "Not as far as I know," she said. "He changed his name a long time ago, before he met Mom, even." Callie's temper broke at last, tears returning while she slapped her phone against her thigh hard enough I worried she might hurt herself. "I don't even care if it was Blake or who it was. The fact Mom doesn't know? That's the worst part." Callie sobbed softly. "She gives me all these lectures on boys and she doesn't even know who my father really is."

Yikes.

"Callie, I have something very important to ask you." I had her talking and, yes, I was that person who used someone's emotions against them in the course of an investigation, though I admit my compassion levels were at an all-time high. I had two amazing, powerful parents who not only loved me but adored one another with a singular focus that sometimes embarrassed me but always inspired my own relationship with Crew. I could only imagine what Callie was going through.

And yet, I had a murder to solve.

She blinked through her tears, waiting. Excellent, I had her attention and asked my next question as gently as I could, hoping she'd just blurt the answer before thinking about it.

"What were you and Elise Steel talking about in the bar?"

Callie fish lipped a moment, cheeks flushing where they'd been mottled from her weeping, guilt creeping across her eyes. "What do you mean?"

Yeah, nice try, kid. "Were you trying to sell one of your mother's inventions?"

I might as well have slapped her, she reacted so powerfully, rocking back away from me, mouth a big O of surprise, eyes wide. "No!" She shouted that denial, the word echoing back from the hallway behind me. "I'd never do that to Mom."

Thing was, while maybe she wouldn't, I didn't put anything past Elise Steel at this point. Especially when, perfect timing or waiting for a chance to pounce, the very patent lawyer appeared as if from nowhere, her face as rigid as her last name, eyes flashing anger.

"You don't have to answer her questions, Callie." Elise came to a halt next to the teenager, hooking her long fingers through the crook of the girl's arm. "I'll take you back to your room now. Ms. Fleming. You've had enough time alone with Callie and no lawyer present. I think it's prudent you move along."

Something to hide, Elise?

Callie, on the other hand, seemed tired of secrets, because she pulled herself free of the lawyer, shaking her head hard enough her ponytail holder went flying past my foot. "No, Elise, I want to tell Ms. Fleming everything. So she knows I had nothing to do with his murder. That's why you're asking, isn't it? In case I killed him?"

I didn't comment, seeing the discomfort and anxiety cross Elise's face when Callie went on.

"I'm working with Ms. Steel to sign a deal for one of my inventions," she said. "The company she represents is going to pay for development and my patent while I create the prototype." My stomach sank into my shoes even as my momma bear instincts fired up so hard and fast they left me breathless. "I didn't tell Mom or Teddy because I want to be sure I have it all sorted out first. But I'm ready to sign the contract and make my own way from now on. Right, Elise?"

How telling, the faintly nauseated smile that crossed the lawyer's lips. Fair enough. I was feeling pretty sick to my stomach myself.

CHAPTER TWENTY-FIVE

WHILE TACKLING ELISE STEEL to the ground and beating her senseless with one of her high heels felt about the right action at the moment, I didn't get the chance to see if violence was the answer. Before I could inhale to accuse her of being a vile, sleazy and utterly horrific person devoid of anything resembling a heart or soul, Elise turned and strode off at a clip, so fast I couldn't stop her without chasing her down.

And that would have ended in a full-body tackle to the carpet of the hallway and an assault charge and a jail cell and no PI license, Lance's about-face or not.

So I held still instead, turning back slowly to see astonishment was the emotion of the moment for

Callie. Elise had clearly taken advantage of the fact the teen didn't want her mother involved in her evolution as an inventor to cheat her out of her rights.

What was wrong with these people?

"Callie," I said, knowing immediately the warning edge to my voice was the exact wrong tone to take with the already emotionally distraught young woman. She didn't give me a chance to warn her, running off herself, sneakers slapping on the carpet as she retreated to her own room and, after a short and awkward fight with her key, slammed the door behind her.

Fine. Callie didn't have to listen. I'd go right to the source of the disgustingness and ensure that Elise never set foot in one of these conventions again. That's how I found myself knocking on Doris Campster's door.

Imagine my surprise to find she wasn't all that happy to see me, apparently recovered sufficiently from her earlier drinking bout to be miserable, but no longer drunk. Though, if I'd had to share a space with Robert—one of the other occupants of her room at the moment—I'd have been in a nasty frame of mind, too.

Trouble was, the third person looking rather anxious and hangdog as he met my eyes wasn't helping matters. If Lance Dustin was also here, it could only mean trouble.

You betcha.

"Ms. Fleming," Doris said, not even inviting me

in. "How fortuitous. I understand, despite the fact you were asked to stop investigating this case, you've continued to do so." She gestured at Robert while I shot an angry glance at Lance. "I've been informed that the provisional board is presently inquiring into your suitability as an investigator and that, to my shock and dismay, you aren't even a fully accredited private investigator. And yet, you seem to be the only one of Fleming Investigations present and accounted for. Can you explain yourself?" She waved off my attempt to do so, plowing her way through the next leg of her furious diatribe with the conviction of the self-righteous. "I'm afraid, in light of these revelations, I can no longer employ your agency and must ask you to depart the premises and stay away from my convention."

"Your convention has been canceled," I said, shutting her up but doing myself zero favors in the process. She glared at me, blinking behind her shining glasses, body rigid with anger she hadn't fully vented by yelling at me. One thing, though, when I was shouted at? Made me shouty, too. Funny how that happened. "I'm working under the direction of Sheriff Jill Wagner with permission from the town council, so I'm afraid your order is just a suggestion."

She spluttered, but it was Robert who spoke up, that smirk of his more than enough warning he thought he had the upper hand.

"I'd check in with Sheriff Wagner on that," he said. "Turns out she's contesting interference from outside agencies and the mayor has a bit of a fight on her hands."

She freaking *what?*

Damn it, Jill. Ego or no ego, this was ridiculous.

What was really going on?

"So, you see, Ms. Fleming," Doris said, rather self-satisfied, if you asked me, for someone whose convention was not only prematurely ended but a cesspool of theft, broken dreams and death, "your presence is no longer required or desired."

Okay, so I knew the poor woman was under a lot of pressure and I cut her a little bit of slack for that. After all, she'd just seen her star killed, her precious convention destroyed, was likely unraveling slowly under the pressure, so fair enough. Robert, on the other hand, was another kettle of rotten fish that stank so badly I wanted to gag.

As for Lance? The little jerk showed his true colors the very next moment, squaring those skinny shoulders of his and refusing to meet my eyes as he spoke because he was a rank coward who clearly needed a firm and physical talking-to.

"Ms. Fleming," he said in a voice that shook just enough I knew he knew he was being a total and utter sellout, "if you don't comply, I'll be forced to rule against you and reject your application, a decision that will not only be final, but perpetual."

In other words, if I didn't toe the line? I was screwed.

"As for Fleming Investigations," he went on like he choked on the words, "John Fleming, Crew Turner and Elizabeth Michaud will all have their licenses reviewed with the possibility of all three being revoked based on false filing for yours."

Again, translation. Do as you're told, little girl, or else.

Yeah, he didn't know Fiona Fleming. Push me and you might find yourself on your back in the dirt wondering how your life fell apart while mine turned up freaking roses.

"Ms. Fleming," Doris said, "you're fired." And slammed the door in my face.

We'd just see about that.

I fumed all the way down the mountain to the sheriff's office, only to find Jill nowhere to be yelled at. My inquiries at town hall got me squat, Olivia out and about too. I fired off a furious text to the sheriff who used to be my friend, several, in fact, in between stop signs on my way to The Iris. Yes, I knew texting and driving was dumb and illegal, and yet, I was so angry I could barely see to drive anyway, so I likely shouldn't have been behind the wheel at all.

Feel comforted yet?

The phone rang as I parked in my usual spot, answering immediately with a very harsh, "I'm going to kick your ass, Jill."

The silence that followed made me check the number and wince before I raised the handset again to the sound of my husband's voice.

"I take it things aren't going smoothly at home," he said.

Growl. I filled him in during an epic rant of Fiona Flemingness never before seen in the history of our small and adorable town. I took the back way, around the rear of the annex to the kitchen door so I'd have more time to hiss and spit and rage at my husband about not only being fired, threatened and discarded like trash but the fact my friend—my *friend*—had turned on me, on us, had to be the single most unconscionable act anyone could undertake against another person they supposedly adored and admired and had to dinner on the occasional Thursday night.

I stopped near the back door, breathing hard and finally done—though I honestly wouldn't be done until I'd burned this town to the *ground*—grinding my shoe heel into the gravel next to the patio stones and clenching my jaw so tight I was sure I heard something crack.

"Fee." Crew exhaled when I fell silent, enough sorrow in his voice my own breath caught. "I'm so sorry, beautiful. You shouldn't have to deal with this on your own." He hesitated then, clearly torn while I pulled myself together, hating that I'd just dumped on him yet again and there was nothing he could do or he wouldn't have paused like that. This was not his fault, and I would deal with it. "I'm coming home."

"No," I said. Inhaled slowly, exhaled, leaned against one of the pillars on the back deck. "Thank you for listening. I'm sorry. I just needed to vent and you, it seems, are always the one who has to take it on."

He was silent a long moment before speaking.

"Things were supposed to be different now that we're working together. But in some ways it's more complicated, isn't it?"

"This town," I snarled, jerked back on the reins of my temper again. "It's no end of surprises and curveballs. It's fine, Crew. Are you okay? Liz's case?" Because he had to be calling for some reason that had nothing to do with me being a total failure at my job, right?

"I wanted to check in," he said. "We're working things out on our end, too. But there are still some details your father needs to handle." He spoke so carefully I knew he had to be working around that non-disclosure agreement he'd signed. "I'll tell John what's going on. For now, we're no longer employed in the case in question, so let it go if you can." He laughed then, a soft chuckle of genuine amusement. "Let me correct that. I know you won't let it go and you're going to try to figure it out while doing truly stupid things that put you in danger." He stopped laughing abruptly. "Please, Fee, just be careful. I don't give a crap about your license. We'll work something out even if they rule against you. You can always go to the academy or find another route to investigation. It's your safety that's always my biggest concern. No job is worth your life."

We'd had this talk a few times (hello sarcasm, my favorite), so I wasn't surprised to hear it from him. Still, it didn't make me feel better at all to know he wanted me, as always, to stand down and stay out of it.

Some things never changed. Grump.

"I love you," he said, the silence stretching between us long enough I cleared my throat so he'd know I was still there. "Keep me posted, okay?"

I hung up a moment later, kicked myself I hadn't mustered the ability to tell him I loved him, too. Because I did, of course I did. I adored the heck out of him. And texted him a moment later that very truth.

I know, he sent back. *Go get 'em, Fiona Fleming.*

And that was why I loved my husband more than life itself. Worried about me or not, terrified I'd put myself in a position where my life was in danger (again) or not, Crew trusted me and loved me and knew I would be okay even if he wasn't here to protect me.

Best husband ever.

Just remember, his final text reached me as I headed for the door, *Robert's schemes always backfire on him, right? This one will, too. Love you.*

How was it he always knew just what to say? Though, he triggered an idea that he likely didn't realize, as I entered the kitchen to retrieve my pug and head for home.

There were two people in this equation—outside the murder—who I had, as yet, to investigate. Time to find out a) how the hell Robert Carlisle won his freedom when he should have been rotting in jail and b) just who Lance Dustin really was and why he couldn't seem to decide what side he was on.

CHAPTER TWENTY-SIX

I WAS RATHER DISAPPOINTED to uncover nothing at all about Robert's case, nor any reason why he was on the loose. If anything, the deafening silence when it came to him was reason enough for concern. Someone with enough power to release him had his back and that was more than enough for me to jack up my anxiety over just what my cousin was up to and why he bothered coming back to a town that hated him as much as I did.

Then again, I suppose the fact Rose had remained behind should have been some indication I'd see Robert again. She'd failed to abandon her post and return to Montpelier and her absolute peach of a mother, right? So, she must have had a hint or an inkling that her darling Robertkins (barf) wasn't planning to be behind bars for long.

Which begged the question—what did he have to offer in exchange for his freedom and who cared enough to accept his proof and let him wander free where he was a danger to himself and others?

I shoved aside my bitterness at having zero answers to so many questions and decided instead to pick apart the life of his present co-conspirator and double-crossing pathetic excuse for a human being. Lance Dustin might think he could play both sides and get away with it, but I had the bit in my teeth and there was zero chance in hell he was going to bully me when I knew there had to be something I could use to pummel him into submission.

Blackmail? Never. But a bit of illegality or even some slip of the procedural (which seemed to be his forte) that could remove him from his job since he clearly didn't deserve to hold the careers of others in his sweaty little hands? That I'd take with bells on.

It didn't take long to uncover the fact Lance was in the middle of a messy divorce with his young wife over their two kids and, what did you know? She was a beautiful redhead, which proved to me there was no accounting for taste in my particular hair color and I wished her well and that she'd find her hero like I finally found mine after enough run-ins with the opposite—I'm looking at you, you cheating snake, Ryan Richards.

From what I could tell the process had been drawn out and desperate, financially staggering for him. Yes, okay, I felt a wee tad sorry for him at that point when the court reports showed maybe the redhead he'd married wasn't so reasonable or as nice as me. Then again, men made us crazy, right?

It was getting harder to hang onto my grudge, truth be told.

Tough not to believe, though, his initial reaction to me had been personal and that alone I could take to the board as a conflict of interest. At least, it was something. Maybe nothing. Argh, fine, whatever. I sat back from my computer, cheeks aching from the grimace I'd been making at the screen, having to wring out my hands because the tension in my fingers made me lose circulation.

My worry about Callie continued to surface while I looked for ways to save my own butt, and I finally had to admit to myself I was importing the stress over the girl's impending massive mistake into my own predicament. Sure, I was worried about my license, but Crew was right. We'd find some way around it or another path to the inevitable. The fact I was surrounded by scumbags and cheats, in this case, was obviously taking its toll and I needed to take a step back, reexamine everything and do my best to dive into cool logic and detachment before I had a stroke.

Well, just because Doris fired me didn't mean I couldn't talk to a friend, right? Not that Nicole was such, still called me Ms. Fleming. Still, I could claim I was only checking in on her and her daughter. Thin, weak, transparent, and all I had to work with.

My call to Nicole went to voicemail, however,

and I did briefly consider trying Doris next, just to let her know about Elise and the scam she was running. As I sat and pondered what to do, an email landed in my inbox, flagged from the inventor group I'd been chatting with earlier.

Thought since you were asking about Blake Hughes you should also know he had associates people hold in question. Whatever grudge roamingangelofinvention (real name Angel Gape, according to her signature) had against Blake, it wasn't confined to him. And when I opened the attachment and took a good look at the grainy photo of a photo I'd been sent, I changed my mind about giving the convention organizer anything by way of information.

Especially since Doris, Blake and Elise all looked so young and chummy in the picture marked June 1991, arms around one another, standing in front of a display that was clearly Doris's.

Which told me, not only were they old friends, but it was very possible the woman who claimed to care about inventors was in on the whole kit and kaboodle.

Riled my temper up again, let me tell you because I then realized exactly why it was I was off the case. Doris must have found out I was getting close to answers she didn't want to be revealed. Way too convenient and coincidental—which I didn't believe in, by the way—that I find out what Elise is up to and I get the heave-ho not even five minutes later. Easier to fire me, to make sure I failed to reveal the truth than try to continue to deceive me.

Right, because she was clearly some kind of criminal mastermind. Still, if I was her, and I found out the investigator I hired was about to out me for something I shouldn't have been part of, I'd have fired me, too.

Yes, I was jumping to conclusions, but I was so good at it, it seemed a shame not to let my mind take those wild leaps that often—if not always—led me to the reason and the person behind the murders I'd stumbled across.

If Doris was innocent, fine. But she'd just given me reason to doubt her all over again and there was no way, after the weekend I'd been having, I was letting her get away with it.

CHAPTER TWENTY-SEVEN

THIS TIME WHEN I tried Jill I called her at home, on her landline. While sitting outside her house, knowing she was there because her truck was in the driveway, along with the ranger's SUV meaning Matt was around, too. Just try and avoid me now, Sheriff Wagner.

Just try it.

Matt picked up after the first two rings. "Yes." Not a question, and curt enough I knew either Jill filled him in on what was pissing her off and he agreed with her, or he was just in a bad mood and I caught him at the wrong time.

"I need to talk to her, Matt," I said. He wanted no-nonsense? He had it.

He hesitated long enough I figured she was

miming to him not to hand her the phone. "Just deal with it," he finally snapped, the thud of the handset hitting something hard telling me he'd dropped me in mid-conversation.

Oh no, he did *not*.

She finally did pick up a moment later, though her voice was chilly on the other end of the line, not giving me a chance to speak before she did.

"I can't talk right now," she said.

"You have a problem and I have information that can help," I shot back. "Do not pull this crap right now, Jill. Just freaking don't already. We've been through too much together for you to be this person when I know you're not."

Her cold silence was all that met my bubbling anger, so I rambled on anyway, glaring at her front door, furious but unwilling to let whatever was going on ruin this chance to do some good.

I was short on do-gooding lately, so she wasn't going to stop me.

I quickly sketched out what was happening with Elise and Callie, the information I'd uncovered about inventors and the pitfalls of their particular process, before finishing with Robert's involvement in a plot against Dad—yes, I went there without proof—and Lance's wishy-washy back-and-forth.

Once I huffed to a stop, there was a long silence before Jill spoke again, professional enough, but still icy and distant.

"I'll alert Ms. Powell of her daughter's contract negotiations," she said. "As for Doris Campster and

Elise Steel, their work arrangements might not be ethical, but I can't do anything about it if they are acting legally." She didn't really say that out loud, did she? "Your private investigation company, while now linked to the Reading Sheriff Department, thanks to Olivia and her meddling," yup, Jill was *pissed* and I now had confirmation of why, "is the very reason I argued against her decision, but I'm just sheriff of this town. My word carries zero weight, it seems." Was she kidding me right now? This was not like Jill at all, and her animosity was getting to be a bit childish.

Whoops, did I say that out loud? Apparently, I did, because I distinctly heard myself finish a whisper with the word, "childish" in it, so yeah.

Sigh.

I thought Jill was cold before. When she spoke for the last time—I hoped that wasn't a prophetic speech or anything—she might as well have been channeling a glacier. "Please be assured there is nothing childish about my reaction to what I've been asked to tolerate." Fair enough, but I didn't get to say that. "For now, know that I have contested the ruling and I am asking that Fleming Investigations be removed from all active cases pending my approval of such involvement. And that, if I have my way, that involvement will never be necessary." She didn't pause, wrapping up with her own hurt feelings clear in the short and curt tone of her voice. "Now, if you're actually able to mind your own damned business, I recommend you do so or I promise you I will report you personally to the PI board and you will never practice investigation legally in Vermont."

She hung up on me. My friend, the woman I'd come to adore and admire, who I'd worked cases with and, if she was going to admit it to herself but refused to, clearly, the reason she had her job in the first place, *hung up on me*.

You have no idea—zero, zilch, oh my god none—how much willpower it took me not to march up her driveway, knock in her door and then knock some sense into her. My friendship with Jill couldn't end this way.

Could it?

One thing was certain. Jill was not taking my warning seriously. I was positive about that. While she might try to reach Nicole, if she got voicemail as I did, she'd leave it until morning, just to spite me. Which meant Elise Steel would get away with setting up Callie Powell and cut her off from her creation forever and all because I didn't take action.

Because I went to Mom's, got my pug, went home, sat on the couch with a beer and a bag of chips and cried my eyes out over how crappy my life had become after being so awesome for such a short period of time it just wasn't fair.

Just. Wasn't.

The lodge drive always cleared my head. Wait, you thought I actually went home? Snort. Please. Instead of doing the smart thing (again, not my forte), I did the Fiona Fleming thing and followed my conscience.

Sure, it might mean my license, my career, Dad's, Crew's… yeah, hadn't really thought it through as I parked and strode up to the front doors, heading inside and directly to the elevators, not caring who saw me but keeping my head down anyway. I didn't get pulled aside by security, didn't have Kit or Rose call for me to stand down, made it onto the elevator and up to Nicole's floor incident-free, so I called it a win as I knocked firmly, hoping she was home.

The flimsy excuse I came up with in the car on the way here wouldn't hold up in court or anything but might buy me some time until I could wriggle my way out and, hopefully, save Callie from a huge mistake in the meantime.

No answer at Nicole's door was the last thing I needed right now. I had to go before someone caught me. This wasn't my problem and I'd been told to back off. If Callie was stubborn enough and stupid enough to fall for Elise's lies, that was her problem, right? She was old enough to make her own mistakes. Heaven knew I'd made my share and they didn't ruin me but made me stronger. Maybe next time she wouldn't be so trusting, might think or act differently and find the right path.

I had to go. So why was I now knocking on Elise Steel's door just down the hall?

Yup.

She answered almost immediately, clearly expecting someone. Callie? Possibly, though her face instantly twisted in guilt and then anger as she realized she wasn't going to win, not this time.

I shouldered my way into her room and glanced down at the bed, noting the contract she'd laid out, knew I was right, that Callie would be showing up any second now, spinning to confront Elise while she crossed her arms over her chest and glared at me.

"I know what you're up to," I said.

"Do you." She didn't move but she did go on. "What would that be, exactly?"

"You're stealing Callie's invention in favor of a corporation that hired you to squash her creation."

Clear enough for you, Elise?

She looked like she was going to argue before she gusted an exhale and shrugged, arms dropping to her sides, quick, angry strides carrying her to the bed where she assembled the contract and tapped the pages into alignment. "I'm not doing anything illegal," she said. "The company wanted to just copycat her, but I talked them into at least paying her something. They didn't want her invention to come out, hated the idea of having to manufacture their own version, so it appealed to them."

"What is it?" I didn't need to know, but my curiosity was getting the better of me.

"A bicycle seat design," Elise shrugged. "Takes all pressure off the spine, the pelvis, the thighs. It's ingenious, actually, though expensive to manufacture and would have forced my client to expend a great deal of money to copy."

"Way easier to squash it," I said. "Why not just let her try to find a way to make it if it's so costly?"

"I'm just the messenger," Elise said. "All I know

is someone contacted me and told me she'd filed the initial application. Said they wanted it handled." Which meant they had someone, an insider, in the patent office or the means to hack the system. Nice. Was there no end to the corruption? "I'm handling it."

"I thought you were here to represent inventors," I said. "What do you think the group will think when they find out you're on the other side?"

Elise shrugged. "This is my first deal like this in years," she said. "I'll cover it up, no one will know, and I'll move on."

"Unless Callie makes a stink," I said. "And Nicole. Which they will." Oh, how I wished this was tied to Blake's death. How lovely to be able to call Jill and tell her I'd solved her murder, too. Wait, maybe I still could. "Did Blake find out what you were up to? Is that why you killed him?"

I knew better the moment Elise began to laugh.

"Who do you think got me into this racket in the first place?" Elise's faint smile had a hint of hate in it. "I had no reason to kill Blake. We were partners."

CHAPTER TWENTY-EIGHT

"**H**E WAS PART OF your scam?" I shouldn't have been surprised, I suppose, except Elise's smirk told me I wasn't getting the whole story just yet.

"In more ways than one." She sat delicately in the chair beside the standard hotel room desk, setting the papers aside, one hand settling on them possessively. "He and I had been having an affair for years." She said it so casually I actually felt for Blake's annoying wife for a moment.

"Classy," I said. "You knew about the life insurance policy?"

Elise laughed at that. "I know about it," she said. "It won't get Isobel anywhere, however. If she checks the final clauses carefully, she'll discover her rights are circumvented by that of his executor."

The slimy witch. "You," I said.

Elise nodded. "Exactly."

"I'm not so sure that's something you should be telling anyone." She might have been clever enough to fool Blake's wife, but she wasn't making all the connections, was she? "Considering the beneficiary of that policy has an excellent motive for murder."

She finally blanched, shook her head, paling out before she inhaled sharply. "I didn't kill him."

"And I'm supposed to believe you," I said, "seeing as you're such an honest person, so trustworthy and everything."

Elise swallowed hard, gaze darting to the door and back again. Was she planning to run or something? Was that guilt, then, or simply a sense of self-preservation she had to be in firm control of considering what she did for a living?

"Blake kept me in the best down low about new inventions," she said, clearly desperate to prove herself. She reached for her briefcase, pulled out a sheet of paper, handed it to me. It seemed to be official patent office stationery, and the bottom byline was none other than B.M. Howatt. So, Blake was doing double duty as a clerk, was he? Or pretending to be if this was online information. "He was a goldmine." She flinched then. "We had an arrangement. I had no reason to kill him."

"So why the insurance policy?" I kept the sheet she'd given me, Callie Powell's name on it. Maybe I could warn the rest of those listed, as well, given a bit of time to hunt them down. If I had my way, Elise had ripped off her last inventor.

She hesitated before caving in, face crumpling, seriously nervous now, hands wringing together. "He was going to fake his own death," she said. "He still had all of his identification papers from changing his name and was going to use them to relocate, after I claimed the money." Elise bit her lower lip, looking up at me like she knew this made her look guilty. Did it ever. Cut out the middleman and keep everything? Who knew what she was capable of? "We were going to start over. He was worried he'd get caught eventually, and I know my time as an effective source for corporations was coming to an end. The internet makes it so hard to hide anything these days." She actually had the nerve to sound frustrated by that.

"Right," I said, all dry, all the time, "it's getting so an honest criminal can't make a living."

Elise's expression flattened out, but she didn't lose her anxiety. "I'm not saying what I did was right, but I did it and it's over. But I swear I had nothing to do with Blake's death. We were finally going to be together."

She sounded broken-hearted by that, though I wasn't about to let her off the hook. Crocodile tears were easy to muster when you were cornered and had nowhere to turn.

"Was Doris in on what you're doing?" I could get that out of her, at least.

Elise shook her head instantly. "Doris had no idea what I was up to, what Blake was doing. She'd never allow us to participate if she did."

"But she let Gavin sponsor," I said. "Isn't what he does unethical enough?"

Elise shrugged like she didn't know what to say. "I guess she has a line she won't cross. Gavin isn't it."

"You three were very good friends once upon a time," I said. "You, Blake, Doris. Correct?"

Elise sighed deeply. "Once," she said. "When Doris was a fresh-faced inventor and Blake had his own hopes. But it didn't last. We all came about our old disillusionments in our own ways, enough to shake us apart. Until that is, Blake and I found common ground again."

I just bet they did.

"If Doris finds out, she'll never forgive me. Not after—" Elise stopped herself, shook her head in a sharp little motion. "It doesn't matter now." Her voice had lost the power and presence it usually carried, so soft, almost lost.

"You're going to rip up that contract," I said, pointing at the papers under her hand, "and leave Callie Powell alone. Do I make myself clear?"

Elise didn't comment, sullen but seemingly compliant enough. "I've outstayed my welcome anyway," she said.

"I'm not done with you," I shot back, heading for her door. "You'll be hearing from the sheriff's department about that little clause of yours in Blake's insurance policy along with this list of clients you planned to take advantage of. I have a feeling you're in for a very uncomfortable time of things, Ms. Steel, and I have zero sympathy for you."

She just sat there and watched me go, though my triumphant exit was capped by, with the closing of her door behind me, a deep sigh and further frustration that my only real connection to the sheriff's department wanted nothing to do with me despite years of friendship and camaraderie.

Why, Jill? Why now, of all times, did you choose to turn into a jerk?

I was just turning to return to Nicole's room, hoping to catch her now that I'd had a chance to speak with Elise, only to find I wasn't alone in the corridor. Just my luck, Rose Norton stood watching, smiling her nasty little smile that shrieked delight at catching me here.

"You're not supposed to be involved in the investigation anymore." She made that sound like she was going to run home to Mommy and tell her I needed to be punished. The fact Jill had clearly rescinded her desk duty orders wasn't helping matters.

"I'm not here for the investigation," I shot back, striding past her, tucking the sheet I'd taken from Elise into my pocket, wrinkling it excessively in the process but having no other choice.

"Don't play games with me, Fiona Fleming." She had the nerve to grab my arm, turn me around when I tried to walk past her. She let go immediately when I stared her down, not with anger, but with Dad's best deadpan that always won more arguments than

PATTI LARSEN

it started. "I know you're poking your nose in where it's not wanted, just like always."

Okay, time to pull out the weak excuse I'd worked out on my way here. "For your information," I said, tossing my head, happy I'd left my hair down today because doing so meant my thick, red mane was free to whip around and hopefully take her eye out in the process, "I'm here helping Daisy with her wedding plans."

Oh, Fee. It sounded way more plausible in the car.

Considering the fact Rose hated her half-sister more than life itself, I couldn't have chosen a more powerful—and inciting—subject to dangle in front of the deputy's nose. Her sunken face flushed dark red before she spun and headed for the elevator.

"I'm telling Sheriff Wagner you're here," she shot back at me, the doors dinging instantly, opening the way to her, which meant she'd come up here just to find me, knew I'd been here all along. "Just wait and see what happens!"

I wasn't holding my breath, let Rose go. Watched as the doors closed and instantly b-lined for Nicole's door, knowing I was out of time but that I absolutely had to act, or I'd never forgive myself.

This time, luck was on my side. A moment after I knocked in a slightly frantic pattern on her door, Nicole herself answered and gaped as I pushed past her into her room, looking around, a little frantic.

"Where's Callie?" Relax, Fee. I'd just left Elise, so there was no way she could be with the girl.

204

Nicole's worry woke instantly at the question. "What's wrong? Is Callie okay?"

"No," I said. "We have to find her and talk to her. She's made a deal with the devil." I handed over the sheet to her mother, watched Nicole unfold it, smooth it out, start at the sight of Callie's name, look up in surprise and wonder and then fear as I went on. "She's going to sign her first invention away if we don't find her right now."

CHAPTER TWENTY-NINE

WE DIDN'T HAVE TO go far to find Callie, though I was gratified she was in her room rather than Elise's when Nicole knocked on the way between their spaces.

Callie didn't want to listen. Callie defended the patent lawyer while I showed her the sheet of paper with her name on it. Callie refused to trust me over the woman she'd been talking to for months since she'd filed her initial paperwork.

It wasn't until I showed her the chatroom conversations on my phone, the detailed, in-depth article written by her own mother, that Callie finally believed me.

She sat on the end of her bed and cried into her hands while Nicole took a ginger seat next to her, arm sliding around her daughter's shoulders, a welcome embrace at last. I stayed to one side, keeping quiet and letting them hash out what they needed to, hoping the conversation I overheard might exonerate the both of them so I could move on and find the real killer.

No, I wasn't quitting. Were you kidding me right now?

"Sweetie," Nicole said, Callie's head now on her shoulder, "I'm so sorry. I had no idea. I wish you'd told me you were working on your own ideas."

"Not ideas, Mom." Callie reacted badly to her mother's choice of words, standing abruptly, tossing her hands in the air, clearly lacking some validation she'd been longing for. If Nicole didn't see it, I did, as sharp as the cutting hurt the girl carried around with her. "Inventions. Prototypes. I applied for a patent." She pointed at the paper on the bed as if she could force her mother to see the truth and accept it.

Nicole finally nodded, sad, though. "I never wanted this for you," she said. "My obsession. I hoped you'd find some other form of expression that didn't lead to the failure I've had." Protecting her kid from heartache was an excellent reason for a lot of things, but still no excuse for holding her back. I should know. Dad did it to me and it meant years of meandering through school, dead-end jobs and fights with him that drove me from Reading for ten years. Still, I kept my peace and let them hash it out because it was truly none of my business this time.

Yeah, I had boundaries.

"Baby," Nicole said. Cleared her throat. "Tell me you didn't do something to my invention to hurt him."

So that was it? She thought Callie killed Blake? The guilty look Nicole shot me meant the world. She was trusting me not to turn her kid in, but she had to know I would if it came down to it.

Callie laughed at that, through tears, sat next to her mother again. "Mom," she said. "Tell me you didn't sabotage your own work to kill that jerk?"

They stared at each other a long moment before hugging one another, the truth finally out.

"You two both thought the other killed him, is that it?" I couldn't keep the humor from my voice, almost giggled but played the professional. "Moms," I eye rolled to Callie. "Kids," I huffed at Nicole

Relief was a flood of laughter from both of them, though it really wasn't funny because a man was dead. But I knew now, hands down, without a doubt, neither of them had a part in his demise.

"I thought you killed him because he wouldn't leave Isobel," Callie said.

Nicole's eyes widened, in wonder, not in denial.

Callie wasn't done. "I overheard you, begging him to leave her for you, at the last con." She seemed ashamed of that behavior, refusing to look at her mother. "He wasn't worthy of you, Mom."

Nicole seemed to think a moment before light lit her gaze. "It wasn't what you thought you heard," she said. "I know the conversation you're talking about. I asked him to leave her, didn't I? I wasn't talking about Isobel, sweetie. I was talking about the agent he was using. I was sure she wasn't playing him straight. There were complaints about her on the message boards and I wanted him to know. He helped me once after we were broken up, after you were born. I needed to return the favor."

Callie gaped at her mother before a soft sob escaped. Meanwhile, it was Nicole's turn.

"I thought you killed him because you found out he was your father and refused to acknowledge you." Nicole sniffled a little, still smiling but with grief in her expression.

Callie sighed, shook her head. "Mom, he wasn't. My father, I mean. I did a DNA test."

Nicole was visibly shaken by that. "You can't be right," she said. "It has to be Blake." She stared off into the distance a moment as the door opened, and Teddy entered.

The entire dynamic of the room changed when Nicole looked up and met his eyes and froze in a tableau of shock and dismay. The tall engineer, meanwhile, looked from me to the woman he loved to the sagging but smiling girl next to her mother and back to me again before speaking.

"I missed something," he said.

"You did," Nicole whispered. "And so did I." She leaned into Callie a moment, gaze still locked on Teddy. "Callie knew about Blake. She had a test done. He's not her father."

Why didn't Teddy look surprised? If anything, he seemed guilty suddenly, anxious and ready to dash for the door once more. Before he nodded, heavily but without regret, instead a stoic kind of acceptance settling around him.

"I guess I knew all along," he said. "Blake's not your father, Callie. I am."

Nicole didn't seem as shocked by that as maybe she should have been for someone who'd claimed to know who Callie's real father was.

The teenager, on the other hand, gaped at him as though he'd offered her something she'd never expected and wasn't sure she was ready to handle.

"I'm sorry," he said, sinking to the bed, head in his hands, clearly distraught by the backstory that led them to this place. "I tried to talk to you about it, Nicole, but you insisted it was Blake all along, so I chose to believe it. Even though I wished it was different."

"How can you be my dad?" Callie blushed then, eye rolled like she didn't mean the details of the act that created her but the circumstances behind it.

Teddy sighed heavily, though he straightened, and his face leveled out from regretful embarrassment to a mild kind of happiness that felt like something he'd been wanting to let out for a very long time. "The night your mother broke up with Blake," he said. "She was drunk, so was I." Teddy reached out slowly, so slowly, and took Nicole's hand. She just stared at him, tears rising in her eyes, but she didn't pull away when he gently squeezed her fingers. "It was wrong, it never should have happened. But I've loved you my entire life, Nick, and you needed me." He shrugged. "At least, that's what I told myself. But the next day you refused to talk about it and when you found out about Callie…" Teddy didn't flinch when Nicole did. "I wasn't positive, and you were so sure so I let it go. That didn't stop me from wanting to be there for both of you when he refused to be."

Callie was weeping softly, hands over her face, though the moment he finished talking she rushed to him and hugged him, and Teddy, wonder in his eyes, hugged her back. "I think I always knew," she whispered. "You've been my dad all along."

Nicole's reaction was slower to evolve, but the kind tenderness she settled into told me they might not end up the way Teddy wanted, but the possibility of an odd sort of family was definitely in the works.

I left quietly, hurrying out of the lodge and to my car before Rose could bring in the cavalry. While it was still possible one of the three had killed Blake, I was betting their secrets were now revealed and I was hunting a different murderer.

The trouble was, though I'd narrowed the list down by excluding Nicole, Teddy and Callie, I was no closer to any kind of proof or even solid motive for Blake's death. Sure, there was the insurance policy, but the fact it was his idea… or so Isobel claimed. I made a call from the front seat of my car when I parked out front of the Fleming Investigations office well past regular hours, early evening darkening the sky over the mountains, the perky voice on the other end sealing the deal.

"Why, yes, Ms. Fleming," Marsha Mansfield said

after answering quickly, obviously working as odd hours as I did and far too enthusiastic in her assurance everything was on the up-and-up. "Mr. and Mrs. Hughes did request the policy together. I did find it odd he'd added the executor clause, however, I assumed Mrs. Hughes was to fill that role so I didn't question it."

I hung up from that conversation a moment later, sighing into the quiet of the front seat, glaring out my windshield at a pair of happy tourists strolling the main street of Reading under the pale white lamps, at the beautiful freaking evening when my life was falling into ruins and I was likely on the cusp of losing my one dream to the likes of Robert and that backstabbing little creep, Lance.

If I could rewind and go back and change anything? I'd have made sure my cousin didn't make it out of the Patterson mess alive.

Oh, Fee. Finding all those dead bodies along the way had turned me rather murderous myself.

If only Jill would relent, I was sure her backing would ensure my license went through. But whatever was driving her resentment and refusal to assist or even be a friend to me when all I'd ever done was try to help her was clearly taking its toll on me. I hadn't expected to lose her of all people over this.

Discouraged and frustrated, not knowing what to do from here and not wanting to call my husband and yet again dump on him, I found myself sitting, rigid and frozen in place for several minutes while my mind ran, and my heart sank.

I hated falling into this kind of place, but it was hard at times to lift myself out of the doldrums. I always prided myself in my resiliency, my refusal to back down when I knew what I was doing was right, but perhaps this time my doubt came from knowing I was breaking the rules and maybe deserved to be punished for it. After all, we'd fudged the truth on my application, carried on as if the process didn't apply to us like we always did. Was my arrogance finally catching up to me? And, if so, what did that mean for my future?

My phone vibrated, distraction welcome from my deep thoughts. I turned on my car long enough to gain a blast of heat, only then realizing the interior had become a rather cold and unpleasant place to sit, loss of sunlight reminding me fall had already begun.

I checked the email I'd been sent and, in a rush, felt salvation in the form of understanding and epiphany wash away every doubt I'd been sinking into, all thoughts of failure and deceit and revenge and guilt gone in a flare of knowing that I reveled in like I always did when the truth came out and I knew who was responsible for the crime I investigated.

Because with that simple message from the inventor group I made the final connection I needed for surety to take me from the depths of despair to elation and confidence again.

It was a short ride back to the lodge, and like it or not, I was going to solve this case. This was what I did, what I was good at. My calling, my destiny, and I didn't care who judged me for it.

CHAPTER THIRTY

THE BALLROOM HAD BEEN mostly emptied, security still guarding the front entry but no one at the back when I slipped in through the rear hallway, accessing the interior via the exit door to the ski lift. I'd been sneaking around White Valley Lodge for years now, so making my way inside wasn't all that difficult.

She was digging around in the only remaining intact display, Blake Hughes's face smiling from the tall banner beside it, her round body wriggling as she grunted her way through a box under one of the tables.

"Doris," I said. "We have to talk."

She squeaked in surprise, hitting her head on the underside of the table, looking up at me with enough guilt on her face I knew I was right, confirmation that email I'd received told me the rest of the story. There were papers in her hands, dug out of a leather satchel buried under a collection of packaged items Blake had probably brought to sell.

"I fired you," she said, not rising from the floor. "I'll call the sheriff if you don't leave right now."

"Oh, let's call the sheriff," I said. "Tell her why it was you killed Blake. I'm sure she'll be delighted to wrap up this case."

More guilt, and sullen anger this time. "You have no idea what you're talking about."

"I do, Doris," I said. "The fact that you and Blake were dear friends, back in the day, Elise, too. How you were inventing then, excited and innocent." I pointed at the papers in her hands. "That the two of you learned about filing for patents together, just like those." She flinched, grabbing for the satchel, tugging it against her chest. "He had quite a collection, didn't he? And not just his."

Doris stood abruptly, jerking her round body toward me, a snub-nosed revolver in her right hand. Well, crap. I hadn't been expecting a gun.

"No, not just his." She spit that at me like this was my fault. Her chin dropped, gaze falling on the leather bag. "He was a thief and a liar, and he had to pay for what he did."

"Stealing what he stole isn't going to help matters," I said.

"Taking my own back will." She threw that at me with enough vitriol her whole body shook with it. "I don't care about anyone else's. I want my invention back."

"The one you signed over to a corporation," I said. "That Blake squashed all those years ago."

"Not any corporation," she said. "One he owned."

The final piece of the puzzle. "I know," I said. The email I'd received? From an old acquaintance of Doris's who'd told me about her misstep, about how she signed over to a company, one owned by none other than B.M. Howatt. "He released his own shortly after," I said. "To great success." His only success.

Doris's body might have been quivering with rage, but her hand was steady on the gun. "He only succeeded because he cheated."

I nodded, doing nothing to approach, hoping not to antagonize her further, heart speeding up a little, though I was rather surprised to realize I wasn't afraid. Too many times on this side of the muzzle, I suppose. Since when did being held at gunpoint become blasé? "You uncovered the fact he was using his original identity to circumvent other inventors. B.M. Howatt."

She snarled but didn't comment right away. When she finally spoke, her tone was flat and empty of emotion. "I didn't plan to kill him," she said. "But I confronted him when I realized who was behind my loss. All these years I believed in and trusted him. I was a fool. But last week when I found out who was behind the company that stole my work, when I uncovered his years of deceit, I had to do something."

"You confronted him?" I took a slow, sliding step forward when she looked away, lost in her past or her guilt or whatever it was that stole her attention. Wrestling a murderer for a gun wasn't my ideal choice, but I couldn't let her get away.

Yeah, not my best plan.

"No," she whispered then. "I was going to but when I saw him Thursday night... I couldn't bring myself to talk to him about it. To give him a chance to lie again and convince me I was wrong, to manipulate me as he has for so long." She shook her head, staring into space, face twisting in grief. "I knew he'd con me all over again. So, I decided he had to die."

Logical choice. For a crazy person.

My next slow creep forward wasn't as successful as my first because Doris snapped to attention, lips turning down into a deepening frown, brows heavy over her shining glasses. "I had to fire you," she said. "I heard from friends on the message boards you were poking around, figured you'd come across the truth eventually. I had to make sure you didn't uncover anything."

"I don't give up so easily," I said.

"So I see." She swallowed hard, hand finally trembling a little, gun wobbling. "I don't want to kill you, Ms. Fleming. This wasn't your fault. And I never intended to kill him, not before I hired you. This has all become just a huge mess." Tears trickled down from under the rims of her glasses, dripping onto the papers and the satchel she clutched tight. "He betrayed me. I gave up inventing because of what he did."

It was hard not to feel sorry for her, despite what she did. "Why set up Nicole?"

"It was convenient," she said, shrugging. "I saw the flaw in her design immediately, Thursday afternoon. It was simple enough to create an overload through the plug setup she was using, to trigger it remotely. Not difficult at all." Killing was easy for her, was it? She sounded slightly dazed by that before her harshness returned. "I knew she would be proven innocent."

"Doris," I said. "Now that he's dead, you do realize the patent goes to the executor."

She trembled, more tears. "I'll talk to Isobel," she said. "I know she'll return my property."

Whoops, so she didn't know. "You'll have to hash that out with Elise Steel," I said. "Doris, this isn't going to end well. You know what Elise is like." Did she? "She's been betraying you, too. All along, Doris."

Doris gaped at me, the muzzle of the gun falling just a little. "He ruined everything," she whispered. And then, jaw jutting, she leveled out, as though some internal decision had been made. "I'm taking my patent," she snarled, "and you can't stop me, Ms. Fleming. Elise Steel can go to hell where she belongs."

Any chance I had to talk Doris down was gone. I

knew it, saw it in her face, in her body language, and if I didn't act now, right now, she'd either shoot me or disappear and I couldn't have either one.

Turned out there was a third option that showed itself in the uninvited appearance of the last person I wanted around just then.

"Fiona Fleming," Lance Dustin said, striding toward me, oblivious to the gun in Doris's hand, to the conversation's tension, to anything resembling self-preservation as he came to a halt at my side, rigid with whatever drove him to confront me. "You had your last warning. As of this moment, your license is denied, and your company is under official investigation. I hope you're happy."

I gaped at him, turned to Doris, the revolver, the absurdity of the moment bubbling a hysterical giggle in the center of my stomach.

Doris, for her part? Had she been thinking straight, she could have dashed for cover, ran while Lance was distracted, gotten away, perhaps, depending on how insistent the young man with the terrible timing decided to get.

Instead, cracked and pushed to the edge of her hurt, decades of suffering lingering like cancer broken open in rage, she shrieked her fury and leaped toward him, finger tightening on the trigger, while I dodged to one side, grabbing for Lance, even as the gun went off with a massive BANG!

Lance went down in a heap beneath me. I ignored him as I leaped back to my feet, Doris's lunge bringing her within reaching distance. I didn't have time to worry if he'd taken a bullet, nor to even think perhaps I might have in the heat of the moment. My only thoughts were instinct as I threw myself at the round and furiously snarling creature with the revolver.

She was solid and well-grounded thanks to her shortness and width, but adrenaline was on my side, my leap overwhelming her. Doris toppled slowly sideways, both of my hands tight around her wrist, the right one sliding up her fingers to grasp the gun. I hissed at the heat of the barrel, ignoring the sizzling pain as I jerked sideways, loosening her grip. Doris cried out in pain, dropping the gun at the same moment, the action sending it spinning away to slide up against the unconscious Lance who groaned softly where he'd fallen.

Weaponless but still fighting, Doris wriggled out from under me while I grasped for her legs, her ankles, pulling hard despite the pain in my fingers from the burn of the gun, the old lady's breath whoofing out of her lungs when she finally collapsed beneath me.

Pinned, sobbing her rage, howling her violence into the quiet of the ballroom, Doris Campster pounded on the floor with both fists while I did the only thing I could do to keep her contained as I called for help and sat on her.

Not my most glorious moment, but it did the job.

When security came bursting in the room, running toward me, my mixed feelings didn't allow me the sensation of victory I'd been hoping for.

Instead, when Ross Mullen and his team called for Jill and I finally stepped aside with the satchel of stolen patents in my arms, I said a soft farewell to my career as a private investigator while the murderer—caught thanks to yours truly—was handcuffed and led away.

Nice job, Fiona Fleming. Too bad it meant the end of everything.

CHAPTER THIRTY-ONE

I SAT BEHIND MY desk, unable to focus on even the most menial tasks, all I was likely allowed to participate in from now on. The faint throbbing of the burn I'd acquired from grabbing the gun's barrel wasn't helping my mood, though it had been superficial enough and the alternative much more permanent I really was fortunate.

Good thing Doris was a terrible shot, though I wished forensics luck digging the bullet out of the ballroom ceiling.

Didn't matter anymore. None of it. Not the case, or the resolution, or the fact I'd solved another murder, thank you. Dad might as well have had a second receptionist at this point, for all I was allowed to take part in the business we co-owned.

For now. If Lance Dustin had his way, Fleming Investigations was on the way out, too.

So hard not to feel defeated, Petunia snoring beside me in her fancy bed, Toby tapping away on her keyboard as she continued on, business as usual while I tried to emulate the dear older lady and her determined belief everything was going to be okay.

Good news and bad news seemed to be part of my regular existence, so I sighed over both while I did my best not to break down and cry on what was probably my last Monday morning in this office.

Yes, there was still a glimmer of hope. I was supposed to hear the final ruling from the PI board this morning, though from the way I'd parted ways with Lance Dustin shortly after he'd recovered from the fall that knocked him out—a fall he blamed me for despite the fact I'd saved his miserable life, the jerk—I already knew what the call I waited for would tell me.

"You are a menace and everything Robert said about you is true." He was shaking, the EMT who tried to check him over standing back when Lance pushed her away, rage overtaking him, though I could tell part of the problem was his damaged pride. That wasn't helping at all. "Tell your father he'll be hearing from the board, and so will your husband. Goodbye, Ms. Fleming." With that, he'd wobbled off without medical attention though I was sure he probably had at least a mild concussion.

Having been a victim of just such a calamity in the past, I hoped he suffered.

Snarl.

At least Liz's case had a happy ending, though the staff meeting we'd had yesterday afternoon when the three of them returned to Reading wasn't as joyful as it could have been under the circumstances. Despite wanting to know what they'd been up to I knew better than to ask any questions. My status and pending board decision meant only negatives for my loved ones. If they did read me in at last, and the board came down hard on me, my failures could do damage to their case.

Sucked, but there was nothing we could do about it, so I pulled up those big girl panties I'd learned to wear with the stoicness of a Fleming and let it go.

I hadn't been surprised to find out Gavin Baker had fled town as soon as Jill cleared everyone to depart. Since he hadn't done anything illegal, he was, of course, free to leave. Still, I couldn't help but hope that someday he got what was coming to him. Karma, while a stern and unforgiving mistress, seemed to be taking her time.

Surely someday she'd deliver a smackdown he'd live to regret?

Not up to me. But I could dream.

I did get to talk to Nicole and Callie, only because they showed up at The Iris.

"We wanted to thank you," the pair of inventors said, both hugging me, Teddy lurking in the background. His faintly delighted expression told me they were working things out and maybe, just maybe, this was a happy ending that could give me the peace of mind I needed to accept my own fate.

Nicole's beaming smile for her daughter spoke volumes. "I'm so proud of her," she said, gushing over Callie's invention, the bicycle seat only one of the number of ideas she'd been working on. "We're going to create together from now on."

Callie's entire demeanor had shifted, from a sullen and reticent teenager to a brightly smiling and excited young woman and I was delighted by her transformation.

"It's going to be epic," she said.

I could just imagine.

They left as a trio, smiling, happy, excited for the future, a far cry from the three people I'd first encountered, and I chose then to be grateful for this last chance to make a difference.

Forgiveness helped more than I expected. Though I struggled to forgive the likes of Elise Steel who also did a disappearing act the second she was allowed to leave town. Gratifying, however, to check the message board and see Nicole disclose Elise's activities, to watch the flood of posts in response, and to know that the woman's ability to deceive anyone else from now on had been curtailed.

Okay, so I was a bit vindictive. More than a bit. I earned it.

Then again, she was the sole recipient of Blake's ten-million-dollar policy, so it wasn't like she didn't get her own happily ever after, even if it came from a padded bank account.

The coolest part? Nicole cited me as the source

of Elise's outing and I received, as a result, a multitude of thanks and offers of assistance down the road if ever I needed anything. Because this collection of inventors? Came from all walks of life, I was told. A lovely network to tap into.

Except, of course, I wouldn't be needing them if I was relegated to finding another career that would force me into a life of pedantic ordinariness.

Argh. Mediocre made my heart ache.

I didn't get to witness Isobel's reaction to the loss of her payout, but I imagined it was of the volcanic explosive variety and likely part of the reason Elise ran as fast as she did. Alicia did call to tell me she was billing the widow for the disaster of her room, so she'd taken out the reveal of her loss on the contents of the hotel.

Not a blow-up I wanted to witness anyway. And made me wonder if, perhaps, I'd be hearing down the road that Isobel Hughes was wanted for murder.

Again, not my problem

Doris hadn't recovered from her fit by the time Jill arrived with Kit to take her away. Dazed and barely coherent, the older woman staggered in handcuffs out of the room, Kit relieving me of the satchel and Jill refusing to meet my eyes or even talk to me, sending—*choke*—Rose to question me.

On purpose, too. When the nasty deputy was done asking questions—okay, I walked away when I was done with her questions—Jill was already gone from the crime scene. My attempts to confront her over the last twenty-four hours all ended with her slamming doors in my face or threatening to have me arrested for harassment, so I'd stepped off at last, heart hurting and resentment growing despite myself.

We'd be having a talk at some point. And she'd be telling me what I wanted to know, or my name wasn't Fiona Fleming.

I almost jumped out of my chair when my phone rang, heart in my throat, pulse-pounding far worse than it had when Doris held her gun on me. That said a lot for my state of mind. The display identified the caller as the board's number, and it took me two rings and several deep breaths before I could bring myself to answer it.

Dad and Crew left their own desks to join me, my husband's frown of worry mirrored in my father's eyes, and I took their presence as solidarity, even Toby drifting to stand with her arms around herself, encouraging smile the final piece I needed to answer the phone.

Whatever happened next, I was ready for it.

"Good morning, Fleming Investigations, Fiona Fleming speaking." Yup, I went for full-out professional, because I was. I deserved to do this job, no matter what rules I bent.

If only the board saw things my way.

"Ms. Fleming," a woman's voice replied, pleasant enough. "Good morning. Thank you for your patience as your license was reviewed." I heard the shuffling of papers as she went on, knowing I was about to crash and burn. "We're delighted to tell you our review of your case has been completed and we've approved your application. With the completion of your sixty-day period, you are officially licensed as a private investigator in the state of Vermont. Congratulations. Your paperwork and identification card are in the mail."

I was... they approved... Holy Hannah.

"Lance Dustin," I breathed. "His report?"

"I'm sorry?" She sounded confused. "We received approval from the board itself this morning. Nothing has come in from Lance on the matter."

He must have changed his mind. But why?

Didn't matter. The young woman certainly had no problem with the outcome. "Best of luck with your new career. Have a nice day, Ms. Fleming."

She hung up while I gaped at my dad, at Crew, the handset heavy in my hand, my entire body limp from shock. I muttered, "thank you," into the now buzzing phone and hit end, setting it down on the desk in front of me, barely able to think or speak for a long moment.

Crew finally broke my silence with a tense, "Well? What did they say?"

"They approved my license," I said. Inhaled. Exhaled. *"They approved my license!"*

Hugs from Dad, from Crew, the crying Toby, Petunia up and barking her happiness though she had no idea why we were so excited, all amounted to a very loud and very enthusiastic few minutes.

Dad kissed my cheek, a massive smile lighting his blue eyes while Crew snuggled me against him, and I felt my whole body go limp in response to the relief engulfing me as much as his strong arms.

"I knew everything would be okay," my father said, winking at me. "I think it's time for a celebration, don't you two?"

I hesitated only for a moment, a twinge of worry remaining. "Dad, what about Robert? Carlisle Investigators?" And Jill. We had to do something about Jill.

Dad laughed. "Let Robert try to compete." Even Crew laughed at that, Toby snorting. "Now that Liz's case has wrapped, Fleming Investigations is officially on the national map, kid. We already have a lineup of new cases because of it."

"And I'll be read in, right?" I felt Crew tense, knew I had a new fight on my hands.

Dad didn't comment, rubbing his big hands together. "I'll call Lucy," he said. "I think a dinner is in order."

I chose his happiness over my new concerns, if only for today. After all, it wasn't every day my father got to see his own dreams come true. I knew he'd been planning big things for us for a while now and seeing his excitement, his joy so rarely expressed, I bit my tongue and let his enthusiasm win. For now.

As for my dreams? I was just getting started. How awesome was that?

Looking for more **Fleming Investigations?**
Inquiring Minds and Death is now available!

AUTHOR NOTES

MY VERY DEAR READER:
I can't tell you how much fun it's been to return to the cutest town in America and spend time with some of my favorite people. From Petunia, Lucy, John and Crew, not to mention Fiona Fleming herself, I've uncovered yet again a delight in the voice of this particular redhead that will likely keep me coming back to her for many volumes to come.

As usual, she's revealed very little about the behind-the-scenes mysteries unfolding without her knowledge, and I'm afraid she's in for a bit of a bad time in the next few books, but, as she's always able to, Fee will win the day, I'm sure.

Thank you for coming home to Reading with me. I'm sure there will be lots of murder and mayhem ahead. And, if you're so inclined, let me know what you think of my other new series, **Masquerade Inc.** and the lead character, Petal Morgan, who I've only spent one book with so far (*The After Hours Deception*) but who I already adore.

Happy reading in Reading!

Best,

Patti

ABOUT THE AUTHOR

EVERYTHING YOU NEED TO know about me is in this one statement: I've wanted to be a writer since I was a little girl, and now I'm doing it. How cool is that, being able to follow your dream and make it reality? I've tried everything from university to college, graduating the second with a journalism diploma (I sucked at telling real stories), am an enthusiastic member of an all-girl improv troupe (if you've never tried it, I highly recommend making things up as you go along as often as possible) and I get to teach and perform with an amazing group of women I adore. I've even been in a Celtic girl band (some of our stuff is on YouTube!) and was an independent filmmaker (go check out the Lovely Witches Club at https://www.lovelywitchesclub.com). My life has been one creative thing after another—all leading me here, to writing books for a living.

Now with multiple series in happy publication, I live on beautiful and magical Prince Edward Island (I know you've heard of Anne of Green Gables) with my multitude of pets.

I love-love-love hearing from you! You can reach me (and I promise I'll message back) at patti@pattilarsen.com. And if you're eager for your next dose of Patti Larsen books (usually about one release a month) come join my mailing list! All the best up and coming, giveaways, contests and, of course, my observations on the world (aren't you just dying to know what I think about everything?) all in one place: http://bit.ly/PattiLarsenEmail.

Last—but not least!—I hope you enjoyed what you read! Your happiness is my happiness. And I'd love to hear just what you thought. A review where you found this book would mean the world to me—reviews feed writers more than you will ever know. So, loved it (or not so much), your honest review would make my day. Thank you!

Made in the USA
Middletown, DE
07 December 2023